The CHINESE WONDER BOOK

A CLASSIC COLLECTION of CHINESE TALES

by NORMAN HINSDALE PITMAN   illustrations by LI CHU TANG

Foreword by SYLVIA LI-CHUN LIN

TUTTLE Publishing

Tokyo | Rutland, Vermont | Singapore

Published by Tuttle Publishing, an imprint of Periplus Editions (HK) Ltd.

www.tuttlepublishing.com

Library of Congress Cataloging-in-Publication Data in Progress

ISBN 978-0-8048-4161-0

Distributed by

North America, Latin America & Europe
Tuttle Publishing
364 Innovation Drive
North Clarendon, VT 05759-9436 U.S.A.
Tel: 1 (802) 773-8930
Fax: 1 (802) 773-6993
info@tuttlepublishing.com
www.tuttlepublishing.com

Japan
Tuttle Publishing
Yaekari Building, 3rd Floor
5-4-12 Osaki
Shinagawa-ku
Tokyo 141 0032
Tel: (81) 3 5437-0171
Fax: (81) 3 5437-0755
sales@tuttle.co.jp
www.tuttle.co.jp

Asia Pacific
Berkeley Books Pte. Ltd.
61 Tai Seng Avenue #02-12
Singapore 534167
Tel: (65) 6280-1330
Fax: (65) 6280-6290
inquiries@periplus.com.sg
www.periplus.com

First edition
15 14 13 12 11   10 9 8 7 6 5 4 3 2 1

Printed in Singapore

CONTENTS

FOREWORD

BY SYLVIA LI-CHUN LIN

My mother was a wonderful storyteller. On summer evenings, when it was too hot to stay indoors, my sisters and I would hose down our cement front yard with cool water. Then, after dinner, we would spread straw mats on the ground, bring out a chair for our mother and a tin of coiled mosquito incense, and lie on the mats, looking at the twinkling stars as my mother told us many of her stories. One of her favorite stories was called *The Gentleman Snake*, a Chinese version of the *Beauty and the Beast*. Whenever we asked her to tell this story, she would first say that we'd heard it so many times that our ears were probably filled up with it. But then she would slowly wave her palm leaf fan and begin the story, complete with interruptions—silly questions and comments—from us:

"A long, long time ago, there was a merchant who had three daughters. One day he was going on a business trip and asked what they wanted him to bring back. The first two wanted beautiful clothes and fancy jewelry, while the youngest one asked for nothing but the first pretty flower he saw on his way home.

["Mom, why does the youngest daughter want only a flower?" I asked.
"Because she likes flowers."]

"The merchant finished his business in the city and found the gifts for his first two daughters before setting out for home. But he did not see any flowers, let alone a pretty one. Just when he was despairing over the likelihood that he would have to disappoint his favorite daughter, he saw a great mansion encircled by a high, red-brick wall, over which the most beautiful flower he'd ever seen was hanging.

["Mom, what kind of flower was it?" I asked.
"I don't know."
"Was it a rose?"
"I don't know."
"What does it matter? Why can't you just listen to the story?" one of my sisters said.]

"He ran over and picked the flower, and lo and behold, a thunderous voice boomed from behind the wall, as a man's face appeared.
'Who are you? How dare you pluck my only flower?' the man said.
'I… I… am so sorry. I saw this beautiful flower and could not help myself,' the merchant replied in a terrified voice, for what came after the face was not a human body but a gigantic, coiling snake.

["How big was the snake?"

"Very big—so big it could survey his whole house without moving at all."

"How did it do that?"

"He sat in his living room and stuck parts of his body out so his head could move around the yard."

"Wow, I wish I could do that—then I wouldn't have to go to school!"

"You want to become a snake? Ugh!"]

" 'So, you thought that since the flower was pretty you could just pick it for yourself?'

'No, sir, I… I…'

'You what? If you don't give me a good reason, I'm going to devour you, and believe me, I can do that very easily.'

["If he had a knife with him, he could cut his way out of the snake's belly and kill it too," I said.

"Why do you have to interrupt all the time?" asked my second sister.]

"The frightened merchant told the snake about the promise he'd made to his daughter.

'Hmm, you sound like a good father. I will spare your life if one of your daughters is willing to take your place,' the snake said with an unfathomable glint in his eyes.

'I'd rather be devoured by you than have you harm my daughters!'

'I won't eat your daughter—I just want her company. I live alone in this big house and I'm very lonely. No girl wants to marry me, because I'm a snake.' The snake was looking quite sad.

["Do snakes get lonely too?"

"How would I know? Go ask a snake."]

" 'I don't know about that. I don't want my daughters to marry a snake either,' the merchant said to himself, clearly not daring to reveal his thoughts.

'It's up to you. Either I swallow you or you give me your daughter.'

'I have to talk to them,' the merchant said meekly.

'Sure, go talk to them. You'll know which is the filial one—whichever one is willing to sacrifice her happiness for her father. Especially after you've bought them beautiful clothes and fancy jewelry.' The snake smiled.

The merchant was speechless. How could the snake have known what he'd bought for his daughters? But saving his own life was a more pressing matter, so he hurried home.

'Remember, I know where you live. So if one of your daughters doesn't come on your behalf in three days, I'm going to look you up and devour you!' the snake shouted at his retreating back before recoiling inside the mansion—a sight that the merchant was fortunate to miss.

["How did the snake know everything?" I asked.

"He was a snake demon," my mother said.

"Where does a snake demon come from?" I asked.

"If a snake tries to be good and study the *Tao*, it will gradually take on human form. This snake hadn't being studying very long because only his head was like a human's," my mother said.

"What is *Tao*?" I continued.

"*Tao* is to become human. Don't you know anything?" my second sister answered impatiently.

"How would I know? We don't learn things like that at school."]

"When he arrived home, the merchant gave the presents to his daughters, who received them with shrieks of delight. Except for the youngest one; she could tell that something was wrong and pressed her father persistently until he told them the truth behind the flower. The first two daughters said they wouldn't go to live with the snake, since they were not the ones who had asked for the flower. The youngest, also the prettiest, said she would go.

["Ha! Seventh can go live with the snake," my second sister said.
"Seventh" was my nickname, for I was the seventh child.
"I don't want to. I don't want to live with a snake. Mom, please don't let them make me go live with a snake."
"They're only teasing you."
"Yes, Seventh can go." It was my third sister.
"I'm not the prettiest one, so I don't have to go. Second Sister will go; she's prettier than me and Third Sister."]

"The youngest daughter was terrified of the snake in the beginning, but he turned out to be a real gentleman who treated her tenderly. They were very happy together. And his house was filled with wonderful things.

["What kind of wonderful things, Mom?" I asked.
"A big, nice Simmons…"
"What's a Simmons?"
"A bed with spring coils. It's so soft, you sink into it as soon as you lie down."
"Sixth, let Mom finish," my second sister said.]

"After a year, the youngest daughter was no longer afraid, but she was very sad, because her father had passed away. Then, one day, her sisters came to visit her. They were completely taken by the riches of the mansion and could barely conceal their envy. So they offered to stick around to help the younger sister take care of the big house while plotting to kill her.

["Don't worry, Seventh, we won't kill you…"
"Shush!"]

"They tricked her into coming to the edge of the well one day and pushed her in when she wasn't paying attention. Then the oldest one put on her youngest sister's clothes. When the snake came in from outside, he was puzzled by the changes.
'Why do you look so different today, my dear?'
'I… I fell and hurt myself.'
'Where's your other sister?'
'She had to return to take care of the empty house.'
So the snake did not suspect anything. But later, when they sat down to eat, suddenly from outside flew a pretty little bird with a beautiful voice. The bird circled above the oldest sister's head and sang:

'Shame, shame, shame! Eat my food and wear my clothes! Shame, shame, shame on you!'

The two older sisters were afraid that their scheme would be exposed, so they quickly grabbed the bird and killed it. They then cooked the bird and shared its meat. But the second sister choked to death on a bone. Enraged, the remaining sister ate the rest of the bird and buried the bones she'd spat out in the yard.

The next morning, a bamboo grove shot up in the yard. Whenever the wind blew over the towering green grove, the bamboo would sing:

'Shame, shame, shame! Eat my food and wear my clothes! Shame, shame, shame on you!'

The sister was both angry and afraid at the same time, so she cut down the bamboo and made it into a chair. When the snake sat on it, nothing happened. But as soon as the sister sat on it, it collapsed, and she fell and died."

There was always a momentary silence when my mother finished the story; then we all went to bed anxiously awaiting the next time she would retell the story. It was a story with a sad ending, because the youngest daughter died, so why did we want to hear it over and over again? Looking back now, I realize that it was not just because of the moral lesson that evildoers will be punished, but also because of the power of fairytales to transport us to a world of wonders.

Like the stories my mother told us, the wondrous tales collected in this volume have delighted generations of Chinese children, who have heard them from their parents, their grandparents, older siblings, or a particularly good storyteller. They could live in a spacious family compound in a big city or in a hovel at the edge of a remote village. There could be mosquito coils and palm fans, or perhaps air-conditioning and ice-cream to accompany the age-old tradition of whiling away a lazy summer evening with a story; the eager audience might be huddled around a fire or gathered on a heated brick bed on a cold winter night. These tales can serve to teach a moral lesson, like my mother's *The Gentleman Snake*, or they may simply satisfy the needs of audiences and storytellers to let their imaginations run wild. We like them no matter what, as children and as adults, as listeners and—why not?—as storytellers ourselves.

THE GOLDEN BEETLE

OR

WHY THE DOG HATES THE CAT

 HAT we shall eat tomorrow, I haven't the slightest idea!" said Widow Wang to her eldest son, as he started out one morning in search of work.

"Oh, the gods will provide. I'll find a few coppers somewhere," replied the boy, trying to speak cheerfully, although in his heart he also had not the slightest idea in which direction to turn.

The winter had been a hard one: extreme cold, deep snow, and violent winds. The Wang house had suffered greatly. The roof had fallen in, weighed down by heavy snow. Then a hurricane had blown a wall over, and Mingli, the son, up all night and exposed to a bitter cold wind, had caught pneumonia. Long days of illness followed, with the spending of extra money for medicine. All their scant savings had soon melted away, and at the shop where Mingli had been employed his place was filled by another. When at last he arose from his sick-bed he was too weak for hard labor and there seemed to be no work in the neighboring villages for him to do. Night after night he came home, trying not to be discouraged, but in his heart feeling the deep pangs of sorrow that come to the good son who sees his mother suffering for want of food and clothing.

"Bless his good heart!" said the poor widow after he had gone. "No mother ever had a better boy. I hope he is right in saying the gods will provide. It has been getting so much worse these past few weeks that it seems now as if my stomach were as empty as a rich man's brain. Why, even the rats have deserted our cottage, and there's nothing left for poor Tabby, while old Blackfoot is nearly dead from starvation."

When the old woman referred to the sorrows of her pets, her remarks were answered by a pitiful mewing and woebegone barking from the corner where the two unfed creatures were curled up together trying to keep warm.

Just then there was a loud knocking at the gate. When the widow Wang called out, "Come in!" she was surprised to see an old bald-headed priest standing in the doorway. "Sorry, but we have nothing," she went on, feeling sure the visitor had come in search of food. "We have fed on scraps these two weeks—on scraps and scrapings—and now we are living on the memories of what we used to have when my son's father was living. Our cat was so fat she couldn't climb to the roof. Now look at her. You can hardly see her, she's so thin. No, I'm sorry we can't help you, friend priest, but you see how it is."

"I didn't come for alms," cried the clean-shaven one, looking at her kindly, "but only to see what I could do to help you. The gods have listened long to the prayers of your devoted son. They honor him because he has not waited until you die to do sacrifice for you. They have seen how faithfully he has served you ever since his illness, and now, when he is worn out and unable to work, they are resolved to reward him for his virtue. You likewise have been a good mother and shall receive the gift I am now bringing."

"What do you mean?" faltered Mrs. Wang, hardly believing her ears at hearing a priest speak of bestowing mercies. "Have you come here to laugh at our misfortunes?"

"By no means. Here in my hand I hold a tiny golden beetle which you will find has a magic power greater than any you ever dreamed of. I will leave this precious thing with you, a present from the god of filial conduct."

"Yes, it will sell for a good sum," murmured the other, looking closely at the trinket, "and will give us millet for several days. Thanks, good priest, for your kindness."

"But you must by no means sell this golden beetle, for it has the power to fill your stomachs as long as you live."

The widow stared in open-mouthed wonder at the priest's surprising words.

"Yes, you must not doubt me, but listen carefully to what I tell you. Whenever you wish food, you have only to place this ornament in a kettle of boiling water, saying over and over again the names of what you want to eat. In three minutes take off the lid, and there will be your dinner, smoking hot, and cooked more perfectly than any food you have ever eaten."

"May I try it now?" she asked eagerly.

"As soon as I am gone."

When the door was shut, the old woman hurriedly kindled a fire, boiled some water, and then dropped in the golden beetle, repeating these words again and again:

> "Dumplings, dumplings, come to me,
> I am thin as thin can be.
> Dumplings, dumplings, smoking hot,
> Dumplings, dumplings, fill the pot."

Would those three minutes never pass? Could the priest have told the truth? Her old head was nearly wild with excitement as clouds of steam rose from the kettle. Off came the lid! She could wait no longer. Wonder of wonders! There before her unbelieving eyes was a pot, full to the brim of pork dumplings, dancing up and down in the bubbling water, the best, the most delicious dumplings she had ever tasted. She ate and ate until there was no room left in her greedy stomach, and then she feasted the cat and the dog until they were ready to burst.

"Good fortune has come at last," whispered Blackfoot, the dog, to Whitehead, the cat, as they lay down to sun themselves outside. "I fear I couldn't have held out another week without running away to look for food. I don't know just what's happened, but there's no use questioning the gods."

Mrs. Wang fairly danced for joy at the thought of her son's return and of how she would feast him.

"Poor boy, how surprised he will be at our fortune—and it's all on account of his goodness to his old mother."

When Mingli came, with a dark cloud overhanging his brow, the widow saw plainly that disappointment was written there.

"Come, come, lad!" she cried cheerily, "clear up your face and smile, for the gods have been good to us and I shall soon show you how richly your devotion has been rewarded." So saying, she dropped the golden beetle into the boiling water and stirred up the fire.

Thinking his mother had gone stark mad for want of food, Mingli stared solemnly at her. Anything was preferable to this misery. Should he sell his last outer garment for a few pennies and buy millet for her? Blackfoot licked his hand comfortingly, as if to say, "Cheer up, master, fortune has turned in our favor." Whitehead leaped upon a bench, purring like a sawmill.

Mingli did not have long to wait. Almost in the twinkling of an eye he heard his mother crying out,

"Sit down at the table, son, and eat these dumplings while they are smoking hot."

Could he have heard correctly? Did his ears deceive him? No, there on the table was a huge platter full of the delicious pork dumplings he liked better than anything else in all the world, except, of course, his mother.

"Eat and ask no questions," counseled the Widow Wang. "When you are satisfied I will tell you everything."

Wise advice! Very soon the young man's chopsticks were twinkling like a little star in the verses. He ate long and happily, while his good mother watched him, her heart overflowing with joy at seeing him at last able to satisfy his hunger. But still the old woman could hardly wait for him to finish, she was so anxious to tell him her wonderful secret.

"Here, son!" she cried at last, as he began to pause between mouthfuls, "look at my treasure!" And she held out to him the golden beetle.

"First tell me what good fairy of a rich man has been filling our hands with silver?"

"That's just what I am trying to tell you," she laughed, "for there was a fairy here this afternoon sure enough, only he was dressed like a bald priest. That golden beetle is all he gave me, but with it comes a secret worth thousands of cash to us."

The youth fingered the trinket idly, still doubting his senses, and waiting impatiently for the secret of his delicious dinner. "But, mother, what has this brass bauble to do with the dumplings, these wonderful pork dumplings, the finest I ever ate?"

"Baubles indeed! Brass! Fie, fie, my boy! You little know what you are saying. Only listen and you shall hear a tale that will open your eyes."

She then told him what had happened, and ended by setting all of the left-over dumplings upon the floor for Blackfoot and Whitehead, a thing her son had never seen her do before, for they had been miserably poor and had had to save every scrap for the next meal.

Now began a long period of perfect happiness. Mother, son, dog and cat—all enjoyed themselves to their hearts' content. All manner of new foods such as they had never tasted were called forth from the pot by the wonderful little beetle. Bird-nest soup, shark's fins, and a hundred other delicacies were theirs for the asking, and soon Mingli regained all his strength, but, I fear, at the same time grew somewhat lazy, for it was no longer necessary for him to work. As for the two animals, they became fat and sleek and their hair grew long and glossy.

But alas! according to a Chinese proverb, pride invites sorrow. The little family became so proud of their good fortune that they began to ask friends and relatives to dinner that they might show off their good meals. One day a Mr. and Mrs. Zhu came from a distant village. They were much astonished at seeing the high style in which the Wangs lived. They had expected a beggar's meal, but went away with full stomachs.

"It's the best stuff I ever ate," said Mr. Zhu, as they entered their own tumbledown house.

"Yes, and I know where it came from," exclaimed his wife. "I saw Widow Wang take a little gold ornament out of the pot and hide it in a cupboard. It must be some sort of charm, for I heard her mumbling to herself about pork and dumplings just as she was stirring up the fire."

"Here, son!" she cried, "look at my treasure!"

"A charm, eh? Why is it that other people have all the luck? It looks as if we were doomed forever to be poor."

"Why not borrow Mrs. Wang's charm for a few days until we can pick up a little flesh to keep our bones from clattering? Turn about's fair play. Of course, we'll return it sooner or later."

"Doubtless they keep very close watch over it. When would you find them away from home, now that they don't have to work anymore? As their house only contains one room, and that no bigger than ours, it would be difficult to borrow this golden trinket. It is harder, for more reasons than one, to steal from a beggar than from a king."

"Luck is surely with us," cried Mrs. Zhu, clapping her hands. "They are going this very day to the Temple fair. I overheard Mrs. Wang tell her son that he must not forget he was to take her about the middle of the afternoon. I will slip back then and borrow the little charm from the box in which she hid it."

"Aren't you afraid of Blackfoot?"

"Pooh! he's so fat he can do nothing but roll. If the widow comes back suddenly, I'll tell her I came to look for my big hair-pin, that I lost it while I was at dinner."

"All right, go ahead, only of course we must remember we're borrowing the thing, not stealing it, for the Wangs have always been good friends to us, and then, too, we have just dined with them."

So skilfully did this crafty woman carry out her plans that within an hour she was back in her own house, gleefully showing the priest's charm to her husband. Not a soul had seen her enter the Wang house. The dog had made no noise, and the cat had only blinked her surprise at seeing a stranger and had gone to sleep again on the floor.

Great was the clamor and weeping when, on returning from the fair in expectation of a hot supper, the widow found her treasure missing. It was long before she could grasp the truth. She went back to the little box in the cupboard ten times before she could believe it was empty, and the room looked as if a cyclone had struck it, so long and carefully did the two unfortunates hunt for the lost beetle.

Then came days of hunger which were all the harder to bear since the recent period of good food and plenty. Oh, if they had only not got used to such dainties! How hard it was to go back to scraps and scrapings!

But if the widow and her son were sad over the loss of the good meals, the two pets were even more so. They were reduced to beggary and had to go forth daily upon the streets in search of stray bones and refuse that decent dogs and cats turned up their noses at.

One day, after this period of starvation had been going on for some time, Whitehead began suddenly to frisk about in great excitement.

"Whatever is the matter with you?" growled Blackfoot. "Are you mad from hunger, or have you caught another flea?"

"I was just thinking over our affairs, and now I know the cause of all our trouble."

"Do you indeed?" sneered Blackfoot.

"Yes, I do indeed, and you'd better think twice before you mock me, for I hold your future in my paw, as you will very soon see."

"Well, you needn't get angry about nothing. What wonderful discovery have you made— that every rat has one tail?"

"First of all, are you willing to help me bring good fortune back to our family?"

"Of course I am. Don't be silly," barked the dog, wagging his tail joyfully at the thought of another good dinner. "Surely! surely! I will do anything you like if it will bring Dame Fortune back again."

"All right. Here is the plan. There has been a thief in the house who has stolen our mistress's golden beetle. You remember all our big dinners that came from the pot? Well, every day I saw our mistress take a little golden beetle out of the black box and put it into the pot. One day she held it up before me, saying, 'Look, puss, there is the cause of all our happiness. Don't you wish it was yours?' Then she laughed and put it back into the box that stays in the cupboard."

"Is that true?" questioned Blackfoot. "Why didn't you say something about it before?"

"You remember the day Mr. and Mrs. Zhu were here, and how Mrs. Zhu returned in the afternoon after master and mistress had gone to the fair? I saw her, out of the tail of my eye, go to that very black box and take out the golden beetle. I thought it curious, but never dreamed she was a thief. Alas! I was wrong! She took the beetle, and if I am not mistaken, she and her husband are now enjoying the feasts that belong to us."

"Let's claw them," growled Blackfoot, gnashing his teeth.

"That would do no good," counseled the other, "for they would be sure to come out best in the end. We want the beetle back—that's the main thing. We'll leave revenge to human beings; it is none of our business."

"What do you suggest?" said Blackfoot. "I am with you through thick and thin."

"Let's go to the Zhu house and make off with the beetle."

"Alas, that I am not a cat!" moaned Blackfoot. "If we go there I couldn't get inside, for robbers always keep their gates well locked. If I were like you I could scale the wall. It is the first time in all my life I ever envied a cat."

"We will go together," continued Whitehead. "I will ride on your back when we are fording the river, and you can protect me from strange animals. When we get to the Zhu house, I will climb over the wall and manage the rest of the business myself. Only you must wait outside to help me to get home with the prize."

No sooner arranged than done. The companions set out that very night on their adventure. They crossed the river as the cat had suggested, and Blackfoot really enjoyed the swim, for, as he said, it took him back to his puppyhood, while the cat did not get a single drop of water on her face. It was midnight when they reached the Zhu house.

"Just wait until I return," purred Whitehead in Blackfoot's ear.

With a mighty spring she reached the top of the mud wall, and then jumped down to the inside court. While she was resting in the shadow, trying to decide just how to go about her work, a slight rustling attracted her attention, and pop! one giant spring, one stretch-out of the claws, and she had caught a rat that had just come out of his hole for a drink and a midnight walk.

Now, Whitehead was so hungry that she would have made short work of this tempting prey if the rat had not opened its mouth and, to her amazement, begun to talk in good cat dialect.

"Pray, good puss, not so fast with your sharp teeth! Kindly be careful with your claws! Don't you know it is the custom now to put prisoners on their honor? I will promise not to run away."

"Pooh! what honor has a rat?"

"Most of us haven't much, I grant you, but my family was brought up under the roof of Confucius, and there we picked up so many crumbs of wisdom that we are exceptions to the rule. If you will spare me, I will obey you for life, in fact, will be your humble slave." Then, with a quick jerk, freeing itself, "See, I am loose now, but honor holds me as if I were tied, and so I make no further attempt to get away."

"Much good it would do you," purred Whitehead, her fur crackling noisily, and her mouth watering for a taste of rat steak. "However, I am quite willing to put you to the test. First, answer a few polite questions and I will see if you're a truthful fellow. What kind of food is your master eating now, that you should be so round and plump when I am thin and scrawny?"

"Oh, we have been in luck lately, I can tell you. Master and mistress feed on the fat of the land, and of course we hangers-on get the crumbs."

"But this is a poor tumble-down house. How can they afford such eating?"

"That is a great secret, but as I am in honor bound to tell you, here goes. My mistress has just obtained in some manner or other, a fairy's charm———"

"She stole it from our place," hissed the cat, "I will claw her eyes out if I get the chance. Why, we've been fairly starving for want of that beetle. She stole it from us just after she had been an invited guest! What do you think of that for honor, Sir Rat? Were your mistress's ancestors followers of the sage?"

"Oh, oh, oh! Why, that explains everything!" wailed the rat. "I have often wondered how they got the golden beetle, and yet of course I dared not ask any questions."

"No, certainly not! But hark you, friend rat—you get that golden trinket back for me, and I will set you free at once of all obligations. Do you know where she hides it?"

"Yes, in a crevice where the wall is broken. I will bring it to you in a jiffy, but how shall we exist when our charm is gone? There will be a season of scanty food, I fear; beggars' fare for all of us."

"Live on the memory of your good deed," purred the cat. "It is splendid, you know, to be an honest beggar. Now scoot! I trust you completely, since your people lived in the home of Confucius. I will wait here for your return. Ah!" laughed Whitehead to herself, "luck seems to be coming our way again!"

Five minutes later the rat appeared, bearing the trinket in its mouth. It passed the beetle over to the cat, and then with a whisk was off for ever. Its honor was safe, but it was afraid of Whitehead. It had seen the gleam of desire in her green eyes, and the cat might have broken her word if she had not been so anxious to get back home where her mistress could command the wonderful kettle once more to bring forth food.

The two adventurers reached the river just as the sun was rising above the eastern hills.

"Be careful," cautioned Blackfoot, as the cat leaped upon his back for her ride across the stream, "be careful not to forget the treasure. In short, remember that even though you are a female, it is necessary to keep your mouth closed until we reach the other side."

"Thanks, but I don't think I need your advice," replied Whitehead, picking up the beetle and leaping on to the dog's back.

But alas! just as they were nearing the farther shore, the excited cat forgot her wisdom for a moment. A fish suddenly leaped out of the water directly under her nose. It was too great a temptation. Snap! went her jaws in a vain effort to land the scaly treasure, and the golden beetle sank to the bottom of the river.

"There!" said the dog angrily, "what did I tell you? Now all our trouble has been in vain—all on account of your stupidity."

For a time there was a bitter dispute, and the companions called each other some very bad names—such as turtle and rabbit. Just as they were starting away from the river, disappointed and discouraged, a friendly frog who had by chance heard their conversation offered to fetch the treasure from the bottom of the stream. No sooner said than done, and after thanking this accommodating animal profusely, they turned homeward once more.

When they reached the cottage the door was shut, and, bark as he would, Blackfoot could not persuade his master to open it. There was the sound of loud wailing inside.

"Mistress is broken-hearted," whispered the cat, "I will go to her and make her happy."

So saying, she sprang lightly through a hole in the paper window, which, alas! was too small and too far from the ground for the faithful dog to enter.

A sad sight greeted the gaze of Whitehead. The son was lying on the bed unconscious, almost dead for want of food, while his mother, in despair, was rocking backwards and forwards wringing her wrinkled hands and crying at the top of her voice for someone to come and save them.

"Here I am, mistress," cried Whitehead, "and here is the treasure you are weeping for. I have rescued it and brought it back to you."

The widow, wild with joy at sight of the beetle, seized the cat in her scrawny arms and hugged the pet tightly to her bosom.

"Breakfast, son, breakfast! Wake up from your swoon! Fortune has come again. We are saved from starvation!"

Soon a steaming hot meal was ready, and you may well imagine how the old woman and her son, heaping praises upon Whitehead, filled the beast's platter with good things, but never a word did they say of the faithful dog, who remained outside sniffing the fragrant odors and waiting in sad wonder, for all this time the artful cat had said nothing of Blackfoot's part in the rescue of the golden beetle.

At last, when breakfast was over, slipping away from the others, Whitehead jumped out through the hole in the window.

"Oh, my dear Blackfoot," she began laughingly, "you should have been inside to see what a feast they gave me! Mistress was so delighted at my bringing back her treasure that she could not give me enough to eat, nor say enough kind things about me. Too bad, old fellow, that you are hungry. You'd better run out into the street and hunt up a bone."

Maddened by the shameful treachery of his companion, the enraged dog sprang upon the cat and in a few seconds had shaken her to death.

"So dies the one who forgets a friend and who loses honor," he cried sadly, as he stood over the body of his companion.

Rushing out into the street, he proclaimed the treachery of Whitehead to the members of his tribe, at the same time advising that all self-respecting dogs should from that time onwards make war upon the feline race.

And that is why the descendants of old Blackfoot, whether in China or in the great countries of the West, have waged continual war upon the children and grandchildren of Whitehead, for a thousand generations of dogs have fought them and hated them with a great and lasting hatred.

THE GREAT BELL

 HE mighty Yongluo sat on the great throne surrounded by a hundred attendants. He was sad, for he could think of no wonderful thing to do for his country. He flirted his silken fan nervously and snapped his long finger-nails in the impatience of despair.

"Woe is me!" he cried at last, his sorrow getting the better of his usual calmness. "I have picked up the great capital and moved it from the South to Beijing and have built here a mighty city. I have surrounded my city with a wall, even thicker and greater than the famous wall of China. I have constructed in this city scores of temples and palaces. I have had the wise men and scholars compile a great book of wisdom, made up of 23,000 volumes, the largest and most wonderful collection of learning ever gathered together by the hands of men. I have built watch-towers, bridges, and giant monuments, and now, alas! as I approach the end of my days as ruler of the Middle Kingdom there is nothing more to be done for my people. Better far that I should even now close my tired eyes forever and mount up on high to be the guest of the dragon, than live on in idleness, giving to my children an example of uselessness and sloth."

"But, your Majesty," began one of Yongluo's most faithful courtiers, named Minglin, falling upon his knees and knocking his head three times on the ground, "if you would only deign to listen to your humble slave, I would dare to suggest a great gift for which the many people of Beijing, your children, would rise up and bless you both now and in future generations."

"Only tell me of such a gift and I will not only grant it to the imperial city, but as a sign of thanksgiving to you for your sage counsel I will bestow upon you the royal peacock feather."

"It is not for one of my small virtues," replied the delighted official, "to wear the feather when others so much wiser are denied it, but if it please your Majesty, remember that in the northern district of the city there has been erected a bell-tower which as yet remains empty. The people of the city need a giant bell to sound out the fleeting hours of the day, that they may be urged on to perform their labors and not be idle. The water-clock already marks the hours, but there is no bell to proclaim them to the populace."

"A good suggestion in sooth," answered the emperor, smiling, "and yet who is there among us that has skill enough in bell-craft to do the task you propose? I am told that to cast a bell worthy of our imperial city requires the genius of a poet and the skill of an astronomer."

"True, most mighty one, and yet permit me to say that Guanyou, who so skillfully molded the imperial cannon, can also cast a giant bell. He alone of all your subjects is worthy of the task, for he alone can do it justice."

Now, the official who proposed the name of Guanyou to the emperor had two objects in so doing. He wished to quiet the grief of Yongluo, who was mourning because he had nothing left to do for his people, and, at the same time, to raise Guanyou to high rank, for Guanyou's only daughter had for several years been betrothed to Minglin's only son, and it would be a great stroke of luck for Minglin if his daughter-in-law's father should come under direct favor of the emperor.

"Depend upon it, Guanyou can do the work better than any other man within the length and breadth of your empire," continued Minglin, again bowing low three times.

"Then summon Guanyou at once to my presence, that I may confer with him about this important business."

In great glee Minglin arose and backed himself away from the golden throne, for it would have been very improper for him to turn his coat-tails on the Son of Heaven.

But it was with no little fear that Guanyou undertook the casting of the great bell.

"Can a carpenter make shoes?" he had protested, when Minglin had broken the emperor's message to him.

"Yes," replied the other quickly, "if they be like those worn by the little island dwarfs, and, therefore, made of wood. Bells and cannon are cast from similar material. You ought easily to adapt yourself to this new work."

Now when Guanyou's daughter found out what he was about to undertake, she was filled with a great fear.

"Oh, honored father," she cried, "think well before you give this promise. As a cannon-maker you are successful, but who can say about the other task? And if you fail, the Great One's wrath will fall heavily upon you."

"Just hear the girl," interrupted the ambitious mother. "What do you know about success and failure? You'd better stick to the subject of cooking and baby-clothes, for you will soon be married. As for your father, pray let him attend to his own business. It is unseemly for a girl to meddle in her father's affairs."

And so poor Ke'ai—for that was the maiden's name—was silenced, and went back to her fancy-work with a big tear stealing down her fair cheek, for she loved her father dearly and there had come into her heart a strange terror at thought of his possible danger.

Meanwhile, Guanyou was summoned to the Forbidden City, which is in the center of Beijing, and in which stands the imperial palace. There he received his instructions from the Son of Heaven.

"And remember," said Yongluo in conclusion, "this bell must be so great that the sound of it will ring out to a distance of thirty-three miles on every hand. To this end, you should add in proper proportions gold and brass, for they give depth and strength to everything with which they mingle. Furthermore, in order that this giant may not be lacking in the quality of sweetness, you must add silver in due proportion, while the sayings of the sages must be graven on its sides."

Now when Guanyou had really received his commission from the emperor he searched the bookstalls of the city to find if possible some ancient descriptions of the best methods used in bell-casting. Also he offered generous wages to all who had ever had experience in the great work for which he was preparing. Soon his great foundry was alive with laborers; huge fires were burning; great piles of gold, silver and other metals were lying here and there, ready to be weighed.

Whenever Guanyou went out to a public tea-house all of his friends plied him with questions about the great bell.

"Will it be the largest in the world?"

"Oh, no," he would reply, "that is not necessary, but it must be the sweetest-toned, for we Chinese strive not for size, but for purity; not for greatness, but for virtue."

"When will it be finished?"

"Only the gods can tell, for I have had little experience, and perhaps I shall fail to mix the metals properly."

Every few days the Son of Heaven himself would send an imperial messenger to ask similar questions, for a king is likely to be just as curious as his subjects, but Guanyou would always modestly reply that he could not be certain; it was very doubtful when the bell would be ready.

At last, however, after consulting an astrologer, Guanyou appointed a day for the casting, and then there came another courtier robed in splendid garments, saying that at the proper hour the Great One himself would for the first time cross Guanyou's threshold—would come to see the casting of the bell he had ordered for his people. On hearing this, Guanyou was sore afraid, for he felt that somehow, in spite of all his reading, in spite of all the advice he had received from well-wishers, there was something lacking in the mixture of the boiling metals that would soon be poured into the giant mold. In short, Guanyou was about to discover an important truth that this great world has been thousands of years in learning—namely, that mere reading and advice cannot produce skill, that true skill can come only from years of experience and practice. On the brink of despair, he sent a servant with money to the temple, to pray to the gods for success in his venture. Truly, despair and prayer rhyme in every language.

Ke'ai, his daughter, was also afraid when she saw the cloud on her father's brow, for she it was, you remember, who had tried to prevent him from undertaking the emperor's commission. She also went to the temple, in company with a faithful old servant, and prayed to heaven.

The great day dawned. The emperor and his courtiers were assembled, the former sitting on a platform built for the occasion. Three attendants waved beautiful hand-painted fans about his imperial brow, for the room was very warm, and a huge block of ice lay melting in a bowl of carved brass, cooling the hot air before it should blow upon the head of the Son of Heaven.

Guanyou's wife and daughter stood in a corner at the back of the room, peering anxiously towards the cauldron of molten liquid, for well they knew that Guanyou's future rank and power depended on the success of this enterprise. Around the walls stood Guanyou's friends, and at the windows groups of excited servants strained their necks, trying to catch a glimpse of royalty, and for once afraid to chatter. Guanyou himself was hurrying hither and thither, now giving a final order, now gazing anxiously at the empty mold, and again glancing towards the throne to see if his imperial master was showing signs of impatience.

At last all was ready; everyone was waiting breathlessly for the sign from Yongluo which should start the flowing of the metal. A slight bow of the head, a lifting of the finger! The glowing liquid, hissing with delight at being freed even for a moment from its prison, ran forward faster and faster along the channel that led into the great earthen bed.

The bell-maker covered his eyes with his fan, afraid to look at the swiftly-flowing stream. Were all his hopes to be suddenly dashed by the failure of the metals to mix and harden properly? A heavy sigh escaped him as at last he looked up at the thing he had created. Something had indeed gone wrong; he knew in the flash of an eye that misfortune had overtaken him.

Yes! sure enough, when at last the earthen casting had been broken, even the smallest child could see that the giant bell, instead of being a thing of beauty was a sorry mass of metals that would not blend.

"Alas!" said Yongluo, "here is indeed a mighty failure, but even in this disappointment I see an object lesson well worthy of consideration, for behold! in yonder elements are all the materials of which this country is made up. There are gold and silver and the baser metals. United in the proper manner they would make a bell so wonderfully beautiful and so pure of tone that the very spirits of the Western Heavens would pause to look and listen. But divided they form a thing that is hideous to eye and ear. Oh, my China! how many wars are there from time to time among the different sections, weakening the country and making it poor! If only all these peoples, great and small, the gold and silver and the baser elements, would unite, then would this land be really worthy of the name of the Middle Kingdom!"

The courtiers all applauded this speech of the great Yongluo, but Guanyou remained on the ground where he had thrown himself at the feet of his sovereign. Still bowing his head and moaning, he cried out:

"Ah! your Majesty! I urged you not to appoint me, and now indeed you see my unfitness. Take my life, I beg you, as a punishment for my failure."

"Rise, Guanyou," said the great Prince. "I would be a mean master indeed if I did not grant you another trial. Rise up and see that your next casting profits by the lesson of this failure."

So Guanyou arose, for when the king speaks, all men must listen. The next day he began his task once more, but still his heart was heavy, for he knew not the reason of his failure and was therefore unable to correct his error. For many months he labored night and day. Hardly a word would he speak to his wife, and when his daughter tried to tempt him with a dish of sun-flower seed that she had parched herself, he would reward her with a sad smile, but would by no means laugh with her and joke as had formerly been his custom. On the first and fifteenth day of every moon he went himself to the temple and implored the gods to grant him their friendly assistance, while Ke'ai added her prayers to his, burning incense and weeping before the grinning idols.

Again the great Yongluo was seated on the platform in Guanyou's foundry, and again his courtiers hovered around him, but this time, as it was winter, they did not flirt the silken fans. The Great One was certain that this casting would be successful. He had been lenient with Guanyou on the first occasion, and now at last he and the great city were to profit by that mercy.

Again he gave the signal; once more every neck was craned to see the flowing of the metal. But, alas! when the casing was removed it was seen that the new bell was no better than the first. It was, in fact, a dreadful failure, cracked and ugly, for the gold and silver and the baser elements had again refused to blend into a united whole.

With a bitter cry which touched the hearts of all those present, the unhappy Guanyou fell upon the floor. This time he did not bow before his master, for at the sight of the miserable con-glomeration of useless metals his courage failed him, and he fainted. When at last he came to, the first sight that met his eyes was the scowling face of Yongluo. Then he heard, as in a dream, the stern voice of the Son of Heaven:

"Unhappy Guanyou, can it be that you, upon whom I have ever heaped my favors, have twice betrayed the trust? The first time, I was sorry for you and willing to forget, but now that sorrow has turned into anger—yea, the anger of heaven itself is upon you. Now, I bid you mark well my words. A third chance you shall have to cast the bell, but if on that third attempt you fail—then by order of the Vermilion Pencil both you and Minglin, who recommended you, shall pay the penalty."

For a long time after the emperor had departed, Guanyou lay on the floor surrounded by his attendants, but chief of all those who tried to restore him was his faithful daughter. For a whole week he wavered between life and death, and then at last there came a turn in his favor. Once more he regained his health, once more he began his preparations.

Yet all the time he was about his work his heart was heavy, for he felt that he would soon journey into the dark forest, the region of the great yellow spring, the place from which no pilgrim ever returns. Ke'ai, too, felt more than ever that her father was in the presence of a great danger.

"Surely," she said one day to her mother, "a raven must have flown over his head. He is like the proverb of the blind man on the blind horse coming at midnight to a deep ditch. Oh, how can he cross over?"

Willingly would this dutiful daughter have done anything to save her loved one. Night and day she racked her brains for some plan, but all to no avail.

On the day before the third casting, as Ke'ai was sitting in front of her brass mirror braiding her long black hair, suddenly a little bird flew in at the window and perched upon her head. Immediately the startled maiden seemed to hear a voice as if some good fairy were whispering in her ear:

"Do not hesitate. You must go and consult the famous juggler who even now is visiting the city. Sell your jade-stones and other jewels, for this man of wisdom will not listen unless his attention is attracted by huge sums of money."

The feathered messenger flew out of her room, but Ke'ai had heard enough to make her happy. She despatched a trusted servant to sell her jade and her jewels, charging him on no account to tell her mother. Then, with a great sum of money in her possession she sought out the magician who was said to be wiser than the sages in knowledge of life and death.

"Tell me," she implored, as the graybeard summoned her to his presence, "tell me how I can save my father, for the emperor has ordered his death if he fails a third time in the casting of the bell."

The astrologer, after plying her with questions, put on his tortoise-shell glasses and searched long in his book of knowledge. He also examined closely the signs of the heavens, consulting the mystic tables over and over again. Finally, he turned toward Ke'ai, who all the time had been awaiting his answer with impatience.

"Nothing could be plainer than the reason of your father's failure, for when a man seeks to do the impossible, he can expect Fate to give him no other answer. Gold cannot unite with silver, nor brass with iron, unless the blood of a maiden is mingled with the molten metals, but the girl who gives up her life to bring about the fusion must be pure and good."

With a sigh of despair Ke'ai heard the astrologer's answer. She loved the world and all its beauties; she loved her birds, her companions, her father; she had expected to marry soon, and then there would have been children to love and cherish. But now all these dreams of happiness must be forgotten. There was no other maiden to give up her life for Guanyou. She, Ke'ai, loved her father and must make the sacrifice for his sake.

And so the day arrived for the third trial, and a third time Yongluo took his place in Guanyou's factory, surrounded by his courtiers. There was a look of stern expectancy on his face. Twice he had excused his underling for failure. Now there could be no thought of mercy. If the bell did not come from its cast perfect in tone and fair to look upon, Guanyou must be punished with the severest punishment that could be meted out to man—even death itself. That was why there was a look of stern expectancy on Yongluo's face, for he really loved Guanyou and did not wish to send him to his death.

As for Guanyou himself, he had long ago given up all thought of success, for nothing had happened since his second failure to make him any surer this time of success. He had settled up his business affairs, arranging for a goodly sum to go to his beloved daughter; he had bought the coffin in which his own body would be laid away and had stored it in one of the principal rooms of his dwelling; he had even engaged the priests and musicians who should chant his funeral dirge, and, last but not least, he had arranged with the man who would have charge of chopping off his head, that one fold of skin should be left uncut, as this would bring him better luck on his entry into the spiritual world than if the head were severed entirely from the body.

And so we may say that Guanyou was prepared to die. In fact, on the night before the final casting he had a dream in which he saw himself kneeling before the headsman and cautioning him not to forget the binding agreement the latter had entered into.

Of all those present in the great foundry, perhaps the devoted Ke'ai was the least excited. Unnoticed, she had slipped along the wall from the spot where she had been standing with her mother and had planted herself directly opposite the huge tank in which the molten, seething liquid bubbled, awaiting the signal when it should be set free. Ke'ai gazed at the emperor, watching intently for the well-known signal. When at last she saw his head move forward she sprang with a wild leap into the boiling liquid, at the same time crying in her clear, sweet voice:

"For thee, dear father! It is the only way!"

The molten white metal received the lovely girl into its ardent embrace, received her, and swallowed her up completely, as in a tomb of liquid fire.

And Guanyou—what of Guanyou, the frantic father? Mad with grief at the sight of his loved one giving up her life, a sacrifice to save him, he had sprung forward to hold her back from her terrible death, but had succeeded only in catching one of her tiny jewelled slippers as she sank out of sight for ever—a dainty, silken slipper, to remind him always of her wonderful sacrifice. In his wild grief as he clasped this pitiful little memento to his heart he would himself have leaped in and followed her to her death, if his servants had not restrained him until the emperor had repeated his signal and the liquid had been poured into the cast. As the sad eyes of all those present peered into the molten river of metals rushing to its earthen bed, they saw not a single sign remaining of the departed Ke'ai.

This, then, my children, is the time-worn legend of the great bell of Beijing, a tale that has been repeated a million times by poets, story-tellers and devoted mothers, for you must know that on this third casting, when the earthen mold was removed, there stood revealed the most beautiful bell that eye had ever looked upon, and when it was swung up into the bell-tower there was immense rejoicing among the people. The silver and the gold and the iron and the brass, held together by the blood of the virgin, had blended perfectly, and the clear voice of the monster bell rang out over the great city, sounding a deeper, richer melody than that of any other bell within the limits of the Middle Kingdom, or, for that matter, of all the world. And, strange to say, even yet the deep-voiced colossus seems to cry out the name of the maiden who gave herself a living sacrifice, "Ke'ai! Ke'ai! Ke'ai!" so that all the people may remember her deed of virtue ten thousand years ago. And between the mellow peals of music there often seems to come a plaintive whisper that may be heard only by those standing near, "Xie! xie"—

the Chinese word for slipper. "Alas!" say all who hear it, "Ke'ai is crying for her slipper. Poor little Ke'ai!"

And now, my dear children, this tale is almost finished, but there is still one thing you must by no means fail to remember. By order of the emperor, the face of the great bell was graven with precious sayings from the classics, that even in its moments of silence the bell might teach lessons of virtue to the people.

"Behold," said Yongluo, as he stood beside the grief-stricken father, "amongst all yonder texts of wisdom, the priceless sayings of our honored sages, there is none that can teach to my children so sweet a lesson of filial love and devotion as that one last act of your devoted daughter. For though she died to save you, her deed will still be sung and extolled by my people when you are passed away, yea, even when the bell itself has crumbled into ruins."

THE STRANGE TALE OF DOCTOR DOG

AR up in the mountains of the Province of Hunan in the central part of China, there once lived in a small village a rich gentleman who had only one child. This girl, like the daughter of Guanyou in the story of the Great Bell, was the very joy of her father's life.

Now Mr. Min, for that was this gentleman's name, was famous throughout the whole district for his learning, and, as he was also the owner of much property, he spared no effort to teach Honeysuckle the wisdom of the sages, and to give her everything she craved. Of course this was enough to spoil most children, but Honeysuckle was not at all like other children. As sweet as the flower from which she took her name, she listened to her father's slightest command, and obeyed without ever waiting to be told a second time.

Her father often bought kites for her, of every kind and shape. There were fish, birds, butterflies, lizards and huge dragons, one of which had a tail more than thirty feet long. Mr. Min was very skillful in flying these kites for little Honeysuckle, and so naturally did his birds and butterflies circle around and hover about in the air that almost any little Western boy would have been deceived and said, "Why, there is a real bird, and not a kite at all!" Then again, he would fasten an odd little instrument to the string, which made a kind of humming noise, as he waved his hand from side to side. "It is the wind singing, Daddy," cried Honeysuckle, clapping her hands with joy; "singing a kite-song to both of us." Sometimes, to teach his little darling a lesson if she had been the least naughty, Mr. Min would fasten strangely twisted scraps of paper, on which were written many Chinese words, to the string of her favorite kite.

"What are you doing, Daddy?" Honeysuckle would ask. "What can those odd-looking papers be?"

"On every piece is written a sin that we have done."

"What is a sin, Daddy?"

"Oh, when Honeysuckle has been naughty; that is a sin!" he answered gently. "Your old nurse is afraid to scold you, and if you are to grow up to be a good woman, Daddy must teach you what is right."

Then Mr. Min would send the kite up high—high over the house-tops, even higher than the tall Pagoda on the hillside. When all his cord was let out, he would pick up two sharp stones, and, handing them to Honeysuckle, would say, "Now, daughter, cut the string, and the wind will carry away the sins that are written down on the scraps of paper."

"But, Daddy, the kite is so pretty. Mayn't we keep our sins a little longer?" she would innocently ask.

"No, child; it is dangerous to hold on to one's sins. Virtue is the foundation of happiness," he would reply sternly, choking back his laughter at her question. "Make haste and cut the cord."

So Honeysuckle, always obedient—at least with her father—would saw the string in two between the sharp stones, and with a childish cry of despair would watch her favorite kite, blown by the wind, sail farther and farther away, until at last, straining her eyes, she could see it sink slowly to the earth in some far-distant meadow.

"Now laugh and be happy," Mr. Min would say, "for your sins are all gone. See that you don't get a new supply of them."

Honeysuckle was also fond of seeing the Punch and Judy show, for, you must know, this old-fashioned amusement for children was enjoyed by little folks in China, perhaps three thousand years before your great-grandfather was born. It is even said that the great emperor, Mu, when he saw these little dancing images for the first time, was greatly enraged at seeing one of them making eyes at his favorite wife. He ordered the showman to be put to death, and it was with difficulty the poor fellow persuaded his Majesty that the dancing puppets were not really alive at all, but only images of cloth and clay.

No wonder then Honeysuckle liked to see Punch and Judy if the Son of Heaven himself had been deceived by their comical antics into thinking them real people of flesh and blood.

But we must hurry on with our story, or some of our readers will be asking, "But where is Dr. Dog? Are you never coming to the hero of this tale?" One day when Honeysuckle was sitting inside a shady pavilion that overlooked a tiny fish-pond, she was suddenly seized with a violent attack of colic. Frantic with pain, she told a servant to summon her father, and then without further ado, she fell over in a faint upon the ground.

When Mr. Min reached his daughter's side, she was still unconscious. After sending for the family physician to come post haste, he got his daughter to bed, but although she recovered from her fainting fit, the extreme pain continued until the poor girl was almost dead from exhaustion.

Now, when the learned doctor arrived and peered at her from under his gigantic spectacles, he could not discover the cause of her trouble. However, like some of our Western medical men, he did not confess his ignorance, but proceeded to prescribe a huge dose of boiling water, to be followed a little later by a compound of pulverized deer's horn and dried toadskin.

Poor Honeysuckle lay in agony for three days, all the time growing weaker and weaker from loss of sleep. Every great doctor in the district had been summoned for consultation; two had come from Zhangsha, the chief city of the province, but all to no avail. It was one of those cases that seem to be beyond the power of even the most learned physicians. In the hope of receiving the great reward offered by the desperate father, these wise men searched from cover to cover in the great *Chinese Encyclopedia of Medicine*, trying in vain to find a method of treating the unhappy maiden. There was even thought of calling in a certain foreign physician from England, who was in a distant city, and was supposed, on account of some marvelous cures he had brought to pass, to be in direct league with the devil. However, the city magistrate would not allow Mr. Min to call in this outsider, for fear trouble might be stirred up among the people.

Mr. Min sent out a proclamation in every direction, describing his daughter's illness, and offering to bestow on her a handsome dowry and give her in marriage to whoever should be the means of bringing her back to health and happiness. He then sat at her bedside and waited, feeling that he had done all that was in his power. There were many answers to his invitation. Physicians, old and young, came from every part of the empire to try their skill, and when they had seen poor Honeysuckle and also the huge pile of silver shoes her father offered as a wedding gift, they all fought with all they had for her life; some having been attracted by her great beauty and excellent reputation, others by the tremendous reward.

But, alas for poor Honeysuckle! Not one of all those wise men could cure her! One day, when she was feeling a slight change for the better, she called her father, and, clasping his hand with her tiny one said, "Were it not for your love I would give up this hard fight and pass over into the dark wood; or, as my old grandmother says, fly up into the Western Heavens. For your sake, because I am your only child, and especially because you have no son, I have struggled hard to live, but now I feel that the next attack of that dreadful pain will carry me away. And oh, I do not want to die!"

Here Honeysuckle wept as if her heart would break, and her old father wept too, for the more she suffered the more he loved her.

Just then her face began to turn pale. "It is coming! The pain is coming, father! Very soon I shall be no more. Goodbye, father! Goodbye; good———." Here her voice broke and a great sob almost broke her father's heart. He turned away from her bedside; he could not bear to see her suffer. He walked outside and sat down on a rustic bench; his head fell upon his bosom, and the great salt tears trickled down his long gray beard.

As Mr. Min sat thus overcome with grief, he was startled at hearing a low whine. Looking up he saw, to his astonishment, a shaggy mountain dog about the size of a Newfoundland. The huge beast looked into the old man's eyes with so intelligent and human an expression, with such a sad and wistful gaze, that the gray-beard addressed him, saying, "Why have you come? To cure my daughter?"

The dog replied with three short barks, wagging his tail vigorously and turning toward the half-opened door that led into the room where the girl lay.

By this time, willing to try any chance whatever of reviving his daughter, Mr. Min bade the animal follow him into Honeysuckle's apartment. Placing his forepaws upon the side of her bed, the dog looked long and steadily at the wasted form before him and held his ear intently for a moment over the maiden's heart. Then, with a slight cough he deposited from his mouth into her outstretched hand, a tiny stone. Touching her wrist with his right paw, he motioned to her to swallow the stone.

"Yes, my dear, obey him," counseled her father, as she turned to him inquiringly "for good Dr. Dog has been sent to your bedside by the mountain fairies, who have heard of your illness and who wish to invite you back to life again."

Without further delay the sick girl, who was by this time almost burned away by the fever, raised her hand to her lips and swallowed the tiny charm. Wonder of wonders! No sooner had it passed her lips than a miracle occurred. The red flush passed away from her face, the pulse resumed its normal beat, the pains departed from her body, and she arose from the bed well and smiling.

Flinging her arms about her father's neck, she cried out in joy, "Oh, I am well again; well and happy; thanks to the medicine of the good physician."

The noble dog barked three times, wild with delight at hearing these tearful words of gratitude, bowed low, and put his nose in Honeysuckle's outstretched hand.

Mr. Min, greatly moved by his daughter's magical recovery, turned to the strange physician, saying, "Noble Sir, were it not for the form you have taken, for some unknown reason, I would willingly give four times the sum in silver that I promised for the cure of the girl, into your possession. As it is, I suppose you have no use for silver, but remember that so long as we live, whatever we have is yours for the asking, and I beg of you to prolong your visit, to make this the home of your old age—in short, remain here for ever as my guest—nay, as a member of my family."

The dog barked thrice, as if in assent. From that day he was treated as an equal by father and daughter. The many servants were commanded to obey his slightest whim, to serve him with the most expensive food on the market, to spare no expense in making him the happiest and best-fed dog in all the world. Day after day he ran at Honeysuckle's side as she gathered flowers in her garden, lay down before her door when she was resting, guarded her Sedan chair when she was carried by servants into the city. In short, they were constant companions; a stranger would have thought they had been friends from childhood.

One day, however, just as they were returning from a journey outside her father's compound, at the very instant when Honeysuckle was alighting from her chair, without a moment's warning, the huge animal dashed past the attendants, seized his beautiful mistress in his mouth, and before anyone could stop him, bore her off to the mountains. By the time the alarm was sounded, darkness had fallen over the valley and as the night was cloudy no trace could be found of the dog and his fair burden.

Once more the frantic father left no stone unturned to save his daughter. Huge rewards were offered, bands of woodmen scoured the mountains high and low, but, alas, no sign of the girl could be found! The unfortunate father gave up the search and began to prepare himself for the grave. There was nothing now left in life that he cared for—nothing but thoughts of his departed daughter. Honeysuckle was gone for ever.

"Alas!" said he, quoting the lines of a famous poet who had fallen into despair:

"My whiting hair would make an endless rope,
Yet would not measure all my depth of woe."

Several long years passed by; years of sorrow for the ageing man, pining for his departed daughter. One beautiful October day he was sitting in the very same pavilion where he had so often sat with his darling. His head was bowed forward on his breast, his forehead was lined with grief. A rustling of leaves attracted his attention. He looked up. Standing directly in front of him was Dr. Dog, and lo, riding on his back, clinging to the animal's shaggy hair, was Honeysuckle, his long-lost daughter; while standing nearby were three of the handsomest boys he had ever set eyes upon!

"Ah, my daughter! My darling daughter, where have you been all these years?" cried the delighted father, pressing the girl to his aching breast. "Have you suffered many a cruel pain since you were snatched away so suddenly? Has your life been filled with sorrow?"

"Only at the thought of your grief," she replied, tenderly, stroking his forehead with her slender fingers; "only at the thought of your suffering; only at the thought of how I should like to see you every day and tell you that my husband was kind and good to me. For you must know, dear father, this is no mere animal that stands beside you. This Dr. Dog, who cured me and claimed me as his bride because of your promise, is a great magician. He can change himself at will into a thousand shapes. He chooses to come here in the form of a mountain beast so that no one may penetrate the secret of his distant palace."

Clinging to the animal's shaggy hair was Honeysuckle.

"Then he is your husband?" faltered the old man, gazing at the animal with a new expression on his wrinkled face.

"Yes; my kind and noble husband, the father of my three sons, your grandchildren, whom we have brought to pay you a visit."

"And where do you live?"

"In a wonderful cave in the heart of the great mountains; a beautiful cave whose walls and floors are covered with crystals, and encrusted with sparkling gems. The chairs and tables are set with jewels; the rooms are lighted by a thousand glittering diamonds. Oh, it is lovelier than the palace of the Son of Heaven himself! We feed of the flesh of wild deer and mountain goats, and fish from the clearest mountain stream. We drink cold water out of golden goblets, without first boiling it, for it is purity itself. We breathe fragrant air that blows through forests of pine and hemlock. We live only to love each other and our children, and oh, we are so happy! And you, father, you must come back with us to the great mountains and live there with us the rest of your days, which, the gods grant, may be very many."

The old man pressed his daughter once more to his breast and fondly patted the children, who clambered over him rejoicing at the discovery of a grandfather they had never seen before.

From Dr. Dog and his fair Honeysuckle are sprung, it is said, the well-known race of people called the Yus, who even now inhabit the mountainous regions of the Guangdong and Hunan provinces. It is not for this reason, however, that we have told the story here, but because we felt sure every reader would like to learn the secret of the dog that cured a sick girl and won her for his bride.

HOW FOOTBINDING STARTED

N the very beginning of all things, when the gods were creating the world, at last the time came to separate the earth from the heavens. This was hard work, and if it had not been for the coolness and skill of a young goddess all would have failed. This goddess was named Lu'e. She had been idly watching the growth of the planet, when, to her horror, she saw the newly made ball slipping slowly from its place. In another second it would have shot down into the bottomless pit. Quick as a flash Lu'e stopped it with her magic wand and held it firmly until the chief god came dashing up to the rescue.

But this was not all. When men and women were put on the earth Lu'e helped them greatly by setting an example of purity and kindness. Everyone loved her and pointed her out as the one who was always willing to do a good deed. After she had left the world and gone into the land of the gods, beautiful statues of her were set up in many temples to keep her image always before the eyes of sinful people. The greatest of these was in the capital city. Thus, when sorrowful women wished to offer up their prayers to some virtuous goddess they would go to a temple of Lu'e and pour out their hearts before her shrine.

At one time the wicked Zhouxin, last ruler of the Yin, went to pray in the city temple. There his royal eyes were captivated by the sight of a wonderful face, the beauty of which was so great that he fell in love with it at once, telling his ministers that he wished he might take this goddess, who was no other than Lu'e, for one of his wives.

Now Lu'e was terribly angry that an earthly prince should dare to make such a remark about her. Then and there she determined to punish the emperor. Calling her assistant spirits, she told them of Zhouxin's insult. Of all her servants the most cunning was one whom we shall call Fox Sprite, because he really belonged to the fox family. Lu'e ordered Fox Sprite to spare himself no trouble in making the wicked ruler suffer for his impudence.

For many days, try as he would, Zhouxin, the great Son of Heaven, could not forget the face he had seen in the temple.

"He is stark mad," laughed his courtiers behind his back, "to fall in love with a statue."

"I must find a woman just like her," said the emperor, "and take her to wife."

"Why not, most Mighty One," suggested a favorite adviser, "send forth a command throughout the length and breadth of your empire, that no maiden shall be taken in marriage until you have chosen yourself a wife whose beauty shall equal that of Lu'e?"

Zhouxin was pleased with this suggestion and doubtless would have followed it had not his prime minister begged him to postpone issuing the order. "Your Imperial Highness," began the official, "since you have been pleased once or twice to follow my counsel, I beg of you to give ear now to what I say."

"Speak, and your words shall have my best attention," replied Zhouxin, with a gracious wave of the hand.

"Know then, Great One, that in the southern part of your realm there dwells a viceroy whose bravery has made him famous in battle."

"Are you speaking of Sunan?" questioned Zhouxin, frowning, for this Sunan had once been a rebel.

"None other, mighty Son of Heaven. Famous is he as a soldier, but his name is now even greater in that he is the father of the most beautiful girl in all China. This lovely flower that has bloomed of late within his household is still unmarried. Why not order her father to bring her to the palace that you may wed her and place her in your royal dwelling?"

"And are you sure of this wondrous beauty you describe so prettily?" asked the ruler, a smile of pleasure lighting up his face.

"So sure that I will stake my head on your being satisfied."

"Enough! I command you at once to summon the viceroy and his daughter. Add the imperial seal to the message."

The prime minister smilingly departed to give the order. In his heart he was more than delighted that the emperor had accepted his suggestion, for Sunan, the viceroy, had long been his chief enemy, and he planned in this way to overthrow him. The viceroy, as he knew, was a man of iron. He would certainly not feel honored at the thought of having his daughter enter the imperial palace as a secondary wife. Doubtless he would refuse to obey the order and would thus bring about his own immediate downfall.

Nor was the prime minister mistaken. When Sunan received the imperial message his heart was hot with anger against his sovereign. To be robbed of his lovely Daji, even by the throne, was, in his eyes, a terrible disgrace. Could he have been sure that she would be made empress it might have been different, but with so many others sharing Zhouxin's favor, her promotion to first place in the Great One's household was by no means certain. Besides, she was Sunan's favorite child, and the old man could not bear the thought of separation from her. Rather would he give up his life than let her go to this cruel ruler.

"No, you shall not do it," said he to Daji, "not though I must die to save you."

The beautiful girl listened to her father's words, in tears. Throwing herself at his feet she thanked him for his mercy and promised to love him more fondly than ever. She told him that her vanity had not been flattered by what most girls might have thought an honor, that she would rather have the love of one good man like her father, than share with others the affections of a king.

After listening to his daughter, the viceroy sent a respectful answer to the palace, thanking the emperor for his favor, but saying he could not give up Daji. "She is unworthy of the honor you purpose doing her," he said, in conclusion, "for, having been the apple of her father's eye, she would not be happy to share even your most august favor with the many others you have chosen."

When the emperor learned of Sunan's reply he could hardly believe his ears. To have his command thus disobeyed was an unheard-of crime. Never before had a subject of the Middle

Kingdom offered such an insult to a ruler. Boiling with rage, he ordered his prime minister to send forth an army that would bring the viceroy to his senses. "Tell him if he disobeys that he and his family, together with all they possess, shall be destroyed."

Delighted at the success of his plot against Sunan, the prime minister sent a regiment of soldiers to bring the rebel to terms. In the meantime the friends of the daring viceroy had not been idle. Hearing of the danger threatening their ruler, who had become a general favorite, hundreds of men offered him their aid against the army of Zhouxin. Thus when the emperor's banners were seen approaching and the war drums were heard rolling in the distance, the rebels, with a great shout, dashed forth to do battle for their leader. In the fight that took place the imperial soldiers were forced to run.

Throwing herself at his feet she thanked him for his mercy.

When the emperor heard of this defeat he was hot with anger. He called together his advisers and commanded that an army, double the size of the first one, should be sent to Sunan's country to destroy the fields and villages of the people who had risen up against him. "Spare not one of them," he shouted, "for they are traitors to the Dragon Throne."

Once more the viceroy's friends resolved to support him, even to the death. Daji, his daughter, went apart from the other members of the family, weeping most bitterly that she had brought such sorrow upon them. "Rather would I go into the palace and be the lowest among

Zhouxin's women than to be the cause of all this grief," she cried, in desperation.

But her father soothed her, saying, "Be of good cheer, Daji. The emperor's army, though it be twice as large as mine, shall not overcome us. Right is on our side. The gods of battle will help those who fight for justice."

One week later a second battle was fought, and the struggle was so close that none could foresee the result. The imperial army was commanded by the oldest nobles in the kingdom, those most skilled in warfare, while the viceroy's men were young and poorly drilled. Moreover, the members of the Dragon Army had been promised double pay if they should accomplish the wishes of their sovereign, while Sunan's soldiers knew only too well that they would be put to the sword if they should be defeated.

Just as the clash of arms was at its highest, the sound of gongs was heard upon a distant hill. The government troops were amazed at seeing fresh companies marching to the rescue of their foe. With a wild cry of disappointment they turned and fled from the field. These unexpected reinforcements turned out to be women whom Daji had persuaded to dress up as soldiers and go with her for the purpose of frightening the enemy. Thus for a second time was Sunan victorious.

During the following year several battles occurred that counted for little, except that in each of them many of Sunan's followers were killed. At last one of the viceroy's best friends came to him, saying, "Noble lord, it is useless to continue the struggle. I fear you must give up the fight. You have lost more than half your supporters; the remaining bowmen are either sick or wounded and can be of little use. The emperor, moreover, is even now raising a new army from the distant provinces, and will soon send against us a force ten times as great as any we have yet seen. There being no hope of victory, further fighting would be folly. Lead, therefore, your daughter to the palace. Throw yourself upon the mercy of the throne. You must accept cheerfully the fate the gods have suffered you to bear."

Daji, chancing to overhear this conversation, rushed in and begged her father to hold out no longer, but to deliver her up to the greed of the wicked Zhouxin.

With a sigh, the viceroy yielded to their wishes. The next day he despatched a messenger to the emperor, promising to bring Daji at once to the capital.

Now we must not forget Fox Sprite, the demon, who had been commanded by the good goddess Lu'e to bring a dreadful punishment upon the emperor. Through all the years of strife between Zhouxin and the rebels, Fox Sprite had been waiting patiently for his chance. He knew well that some day, sooner or later, there would come an hour when Zhouxin would be at his mercy. When the time came, therefore, for Daji to go to the palace, Fox Sprite felt that at last his chance had come. The beautiful maiden for whom Zhouxin had given up so many hundreds of his soldiers, would clearly have great power over the emperor. She must be made to help in the punishment of her wicked husband. So Fox Sprite made himself invisible and traveled with the viceroy's party as it went from central China to the capital.

On the last night of their journey Sunan and his daughter stopped for rest and food at a large inn. No sooner had the girl gone to her room for the night than Fox Sprite followed her. Then he made himself visible. At first she was frightened to see so strange a being in her room, but when Fox Sprite told her he was a servant of the great goddess, Lu'e, she was comforted, for she knew that Lu'e was the friend of women and children.

"But how can I help to punish the emperor?" she faltered, when the sprite told her he wanted her assistance. "I am but a helpless girl," and here she began to cry.

"Dry your tears," he said soothingly. "It will be very easy. Only let me take your form for a little. When I am the emperor's wife," he said, laughing, "I shall find a way to punish him, for no one can give a man more pain that his wife can, if she desires to do so. You know, I am a servant of Lu'e and can do anything I wish."

"But the emperor won't have a fox for a wife," she sobbed.

"Though I am still a fox I shall look like the beautiful Daji. Put your mind at ease. He will never know."

"Oh, I see," she smiled, "you will put your spirit into my body and you will look just like me, though you really won't be me. But what will become of the real me? Shall I have to be a fox and look like you?"

"No, not unless you want to. I will make you invisible, and you can be ready to go back into your own body when I have got rid of the emperor."

"Very well," replied the girl, somewhat relieved by his explanation, "but try not to be too long about it, because I don't like the idea of somebody else walking about in my body."

So Fox Sprite caused his own spirit to enter the girl's body, and no one could have told by her outward appearance that any change had taken place. The beautiful girl was now in reality the sly Fox Sprite, but in one way only did she look like a fox. When the fox-spirit entered her body, her feet suddenly shriveled up and became very similar in shape and size to the feet of the animal who had her in his power. When the fox noticed this, at first he was somewhat annoyed, but, feeling that no one else would know, he did not take the trouble to change the fox feet back to human form.

On the following morning, when the viceroy called his daughter for the last stage of their journey, he greeted Fox Sprite without suspecting that anything unusual had happened since he had last seen Daji. So well did this crafty spirit perform his part that the father was completely deceived, by look, by voice, and by gesture.

The next day the travelers arrived at the capital and Sunan presented himself before Zhouxin, the emperor, leading Fox Sprite with him. Of course the crafty fox with all his magic powers was soon able to gain the mastery over the wicked ruler. The Great One pardoned Sunan, although he had fully intended to put him to death as a rebel.

Now the chance for which Fox Sprite had been waiting had come. He began at once, causing the emperor to do many deeds of violence. The people had already begun to dislike Zhouxin, and soon he became hateful in their sight. Many of the leading members of the court were put to death unjustly. Horrible tortures were devised for punishing those who did not find favor with the crown. At last there was open talk of a rebellion. Of course, all these things delighted the wily fox, for he saw that, sooner or later, the Son of Heaven would be turned out of the palace, and he knew that then his work for the goddess Lu'e would be finished.

Besides worming his way into the heart of the emperor, the fox became a general favorite with the ladies of the palace. These women saw in Zhouxin's latest wife the most beautiful woman who had ever lived in the royal harem. One would think that this beauty might have caused them to hate Fox Sprite, but such was not the case. They admired the plumpness of Fox Sprite's body, the fairness of Fox Sprite's complexion, the fire in Fox Sprite's eyes, but most of all they wondered at the smallness of Fox Sprite's feet, for, you remember, the supposed Daji now had fox's feet instead of those of human shape.

Thus small feet became the fashion among women. All the court ladies, old and young, beautiful and ugly, began thinking of plans for making their own feet as tiny as those of Fox

Sprite. In this way they thought to increase their chances of finding favor with the emperor.

Gradually people outside the palace began to hear of this absurd fashion. Mothers bound the feet of their little girls, in such a manner as to stop their growth. The bones of the toes were bent backwards and broken, so eager were the elders to have their daughters grow up into tiny-footed maidens. Thus, for several years of their girlhood the little ones were compelled to endure the most severe tortures. It was not long before the new fashion took firm root in China. It became almost impossible for parents to get husbands for their daughters unless the girls had suffered the severe pains of foot-binding. And even to this day we find that many of the people are still under the influence of Fox Sprite's magic, and believe that a tiny, misshapen foot is more beautiful than a natural one.

But let us return to the story of Fox Sprite and the wicked emperor. For a number of years matters grew continually worse in the country. At last the people rose in a body against the ruler. A great battle was fought. The wicked Zhouxin was overthrown and put to death by means of those very instruments of torture he had used so often against his subjects. By this time it had become known to all the lords and noblemen that the emperor's favorite had been the main cause of their ruler's wickedness; hence they demanded the death of Fox Sprite. But no one wished to kill so lovely a creature. Everyone appointed refused to do the deed.

Finally, a gray-headed member of the court allowed himself to be blindfolded. With a sharp sword he pierced the body of Fox Sprite to the heart. Those standing near covered their eyes with their hands, for they could not bear to see so wonderful a woman die. Suddenly, as they looked up, they saw a sight so strange that all were filled with amazement. Instead of falling to the ground, the graceful form swayed backward and forward for a moment, when all at once there seemed to spring from her side a huge mountain fox. The animal glanced around him, then, with a cry of fear, dashing past officials, courtiers and soldiers, he rushed through the gate of the enclosure.

"A fox!" cried the people, full of wonder.

At that moment Daji fell in a swoon upon the floor. When they picked her up, thinking, of course, that she had died from the sword thrust, they could find no blood on her body, and, on looking more closely, they saw that there was not even the slightest wound.

"Marvel of marvels!" they all shouted. "The gods have shielded her!"

Just then Daji opened her eyes and looked about her. "Where am I?" she asked, in faint voice. "Pray tell me what has happened."

Then they told her what they had seen, and at last it was plain to the beautiful woman that, after all these years, Fox Sprite had left her body. She was herself once more. For a long time she could not make the people believe her story; they all said that she must have lost her mind; that the gods had saved her life, but had punished her for her wickedness by taking away her reason.

But that night, when her maids were undressing her in the palace, they saw her feet, which had once more become their natural size, and then they knew she had been telling the truth.

How Daji became the wife of a good nobleman who had long admired her great beauty is much too long a story to be told here. Of one thing, however, we are certain, that she lived long and was happy ever afterwards.

THE TALKING FISH

ONG, long before your great-grandfather was born there lived in the village of Everlasting Happiness two men called Li and Xing. Now, these two men were close friends, living together in the same house. Before settling down in the village of Everlasting Happiness they had ruled as high officials for more than twenty years. They had often treated the people very harshly, so that everybody, old and young, disliked and hated them. And yet, by robbing the wealthy merchants and by cheating the poor, these two evil companions had become rich, and it was in order to spend their ill-gotten gains in idle amusements that they sought out the village of Everlasting Happiness. "For here," said they, "we can surely find that joy which has been denied us in every other place. Here we shall no longer be scorned by men and reviled by women."

Consequently these two men bought for themselves the finest house in the village, furnished it in the most elegant manner, and decorated the walls with scrolls filled with wise sayings and pictures by famous artists. Outside there were lovely gardens filled with flowers and birds, and oh, ever so many trees with oddly twisted branches growing in the shape of tigers and other wild animals.

Whenever they felt lonely Li and Xing invited rich people of the neighborhood to come and dine with them, and after they had eaten, sometimes they would go out upon the little lake in the center of their estate, rowing in an awkward flat-bottomed boat that had been built by the village carpenter.

One day, on such an occasion, when the sun had been beating down fiercely upon the clean-shaven heads of all those on the little barge, for you must know this was long before the day when hats were worn—at least, in the village of Everlasting Happiness—Mr. Li was suddenly seized with a giddy feeling, which rapidly grew worse and worse until he was in a burning fever.

"Snake's blood mixed with powdered deer-horn is the thing for him," said the wise-looking doctor who was called in, peering at Li carefully through his huge glasses, "Be sure," he continued, addressing Li's personal attendant, and, at the same time, snapping his long finger-nails nervously, "be sure, above all, not to leave him alone, for he is in danger of going raving mad at any moment, and I cannot say what he may do if he is not looked after carefully. A man in his condition has no more sense than a baby."

Now, although these words of the doctor's really made Mr. Li angry, he was too ill to reply, for all this time his head had been growing hotter and hotter, until at last a feverish sleep overtook him. No sooner had he closed his eyes than his faithful servant, half-famished, rushed out of the room to join his fellows at their midday meal.

Li awoke with a start. He had slept only ten minutes. "Water, water," he moaned, "bathe my head with cold water. I am half dead with pain!" But there was no reply, for the attendant was dining happily with his fellows.

"Air, air," groaned Mr. Li, tugging at the collar of his silk shirt. "I'm dying for water. I'm starving for air. This blazing heat will kill me. It is hotter than the Fire god himself ever dreamed of making it. Wang, Wang!" clapping his hands feebly and calling to his servant, "air and water, air and water!"

"Snake's blood mixed with powdered deer-horn is the thing for him."

But still no Wang.

At last, with the strength that is said to come from despair, Mr. Li arose from his couch and staggered toward the doorway. Out he went into the paved courtyard, and then, after only a moment's hesitation, made his way across it into a narrow passage that led into the lake garden.

"What do they care for a man when he is sick?" he muttered. "My good friend Xing is doubtless even now enjoying his afternoon nap, with a servant standing by to fan him, and a block of ice near his head to cool the air. What does he care if I die of a raging fever? Doubtless he expects to inherit all my money. And my servants! That rascal Wang has been with me these ten years, living on me and growing lazier every season! What does he care if I pass away? Doubtless he is certain that Xing's servants will think of something for him to do, and he will have even less work than he has now. Water, water! I shall die if I don't soon find a place to soak myself!"

So saying, he arrived at the bank of a little brook that flowed in through a water gate at one side of the garden and emptied itself into the big fish-pond. Flinging himself down by a little stream Li bathed his hands and wrists in the cool water. How delightful! If only it were deep enough to cover his whole body, how gladly would he cast himself in and enjoy the bliss of its refreshing embrace!

For a long time he lay on the ground, rejoicing at his escape from the doctor's clutches. Then, as the fever began to rise again, he sprang up with a determined cry, "What am I waiting for? I will do it. There's no one to prevent me, and it will do me a world of good. I will cast myself head first into the fish-pond. It is not deep enough near the shore to drown me if I should be too weak to swim, and I am sure it will restore me to strength and health."

He hastened along the little stream, almost running in his eagerness to reach the deeper water of the pond. He was like some small schoolboy who had escaped from the watchful eye of the master and run out to play in a forbidden spot.

Hark! Was that a servant calling? Had Wang discovered the absence of his employer? Would he sound the alarm, and would the whole place soon be alive with men searching for the fever-stricken patient?

With one last sigh of satisfaction Li flung himself, clothes and all, into the quiet waters of the fish-pond. Now Li had been brought up in Fujian province on the seashore, and was a skilful swimmer. He dived and splashed to his heart's content, then floated on the surface. "It takes me back to my boyhood," he cried, "why, oh why, is it not the fashion to swim? I'd love to live in the water all the time and yet some of my countrymen are even more afraid than a cat of getting their feet wet. As for me, I'd give anything to stay here for ever."

"You would, eh?" chuckled a hoarse voice just under him, and then there was a sort of wheezing sound, followed by a loud burst of laughter. Mr. Li jumped as if an arrow had struck him, but when he noticed the fat, ugly monster below, his fear turned into anger. "Look here, what do you mean by giving a fellow such a start! Don't you know what the Classics say about such rudeness?"

The giant fish laughed all the louder. "What time do you suppose I have for Classics? You make me laugh until I cry!"

"But you must answer my question," cried Mr. Li, more and more persistently, forgetting for the moment that he was not trying some poor culprit for a petty crime. "Why did you laugh? Speak out at once, fellow!"

"Well, since you are such a saucy piece," roared the other, "I will tell you. It was because you awkward creatures, who call yourselves men, the most highly civilized beings in the world, always think you understand a thing fully when you have only just found out how to do it."

"You are talking about the island dwarfs, the Japanese," interrupted Mr. Li, "We Chinese seldom undertake to do anything new."

"Just hear the man!" chuckled the fish. "Now, fancy your wishing to stay in the water for ever! What do you know about water? Why you're not even provided with the proper equipment for swimming. What would you do if you really lived here always?"

"What am I doing now?" spluttered Mr. Li, so angry that he sucked in a mouthful of water before he knew it.

"Floundering," retorted the other.

"Don't you see me swimming? Are those big eyes of yours made of glass?"

"Yes, I see you all right," guffawed the fish, "that's just it! I see you too well. Why you tumble about as awkwardly as a water buffalo wallowing in a mud puddle!"

Now, as Mr. Li had always considered himself an expert in water sports, he was, by this time, speechless with rage, and all he could do was to paddle feebly around and around with strokes just strong enough to keep himself from sinking.

"Then, too," continued the fish, more and more calm as the other lost his temper, "you have a very poor arrangement for breathing. If I am not mistaken, at the bottom of this pond you would find yourself worse off than I should be at the top of a palm tree. What would you do to keep yourself from starving? Do you think it would be convenient if you had to flop yourself out on to the land every time you wanted a bite to eat? And yet, being a man, I doubt seriously if you would be content to take the proper food for fishes. You have hardly a single feature that would make you contented if you were to join an under-water school. Look at your clothes, too, water-soaked and heavy. Do you think them suitable to protect you from cold and sickness? Nature forgot to give you any scales. Now I'm going to tell you a joke, so you must be sure to laugh. Fishes are like grocery shops—always judged by their scales. As you haven't a sign of a scale, how will people judge you? See the point, eh? Nature gave you a skin, but forgot the outer covering, except, perhaps at the ends of your fingers and your toes You surely see by this time why I consider your idea ridiculous?"

Sure enough, in spite of his recent severe attack of fever, Mr. Li had really cooled completely off. He had never understood before what great disadvantages there were connected with being a man. Why not make use of this chance acquaintance, find out from him how to get rid of that miserable possession he had called his manhood, and gain the delights that only a fish can have? "Then, are you indeed contented with your lot?" he asked finally. "Are there not moments when you would prefer to be a man?"

"I, a man!" thundered the other, lashing the water with his tail. "How dare you suggest such a disgraceful change! Can it be that you do not know my rank? Why, my fellow, you behold in me a favorite nephew of the king!"

"Then, may it please your lordship," said Mr. Li, softly, "I should be exceedingly grateful if you would speak a kind word for me to your master. Do you think it possible that he could change me in some manner into a fish and accept me as a subject?"

"Of course!" replied the other, "all things are possible to the king. Know you not that my sovereign is a loyal descendant of the great water dragon, and, as such, can never die, but lives on and on and on, for ever and ever and ever, like the ruling house of Japan?"

"Oh, oh!" gasped Mr. Li, "even the Son of Heaven, our most worshipful emperor, cannot boast of such long years. Yes, I would give my fortune to be a follower of your imperial master."

"Then follow me," laughed the other, starting off at a rate that made the water hiss and boil for ten feet around him.

Mr. Li struggled vainly to keep up. If he had thought himself a good swimmer, he now saw his mistake and every bit of remaining pride was torn to tatters. "Please wait a moment," he cried out politely, "I beg of you to remember that I am only a man!"

"Pardon me," replied the other, "it was stupid of me to forget, especially as I had just been talking about it."

Soon they reached a sheltered inlet at the farther side of the pond. There Mr. Li saw a gigantic carp idly floating about in a shallow pool, and then lazily flirting his huge tail or fluttering his fins proudly from side to side. Attendant courtiers darted hither and thither, ready to do the master's slightest bidding. One of them, splendidly attired in royal scarlet, announced, with a downward flip of the head, the approach of the king's nephew who was leading Mr. Li to an audience with his Majesty.

"Whom have you here, my lad?" began the ruler, as his nephew, hesitating for words to explain his strange request, moved his fins nervously backwards and forwards. "Strange company, it seems to me, you are keeping these days."

"Only a poor man, most royal sir," replied the other, "who beseeches your Highness to grant him your gracious favor."

> "When man asks favor of a fish,
> 'Tis hard to penetrate his wish—
> He often seeks a lordly dish
> To serve upon his table,"

repeated the king, smiling. "And yet, nephew, you think this fellow is really peaceably inclined and is not coming among us as a spy?"

Before his friend could answer, Mr. Li had cast himself upon his knees in the shallow water, before the noble carp, and bowed thrice, until his face was daubed with mud from the bottom of the pool. "Indeed, your Majesty, I am only a poor mortal who seeks your kindly grace. If you would but consent to receive me into your school of fishes. I would for ever be your ardent admirer and your lowly slave."

"In sooth, the fellow talks as if in earnest," remarked the king, after a moment's reflection, "and though the request is, perhaps, the strangest to which I have ever listened, I really see no reason why I should not turn a fishly ear. But, have the goodness first to cease your bowing. You are stirring up enough mud to plaster the royal palace of a shark."

Poor Li blushing at the monarch's reproof, waited patiently for the answer to his request.

"Very well, so be it," cried the king impulsively, "your wish is granted. Sir Trout," turning to one of his courtiers, "bring hither a fish-skin of proper size for this ambitious fellow."

No sooner said than done. The fish-skin was slipped over Mr. Li's head, and his whole body was soon tucked snugly away in the scaly coat. Only his arms remained uncovered. In the twinkling of an eye Li felt sharp pains shoot through every part of his body. His arms began to shrivel up and his hands changed little by little until they made an excellent pair of fins, just as good as those of the king himself. As for his legs and feet, they suddenly began to stick together until, wriggle as he would, Li could not separate them. "Ah, ha!" thought he, "my kicking days are over, for my toes are now turned into a first-class tail."

"Not so fast," laughed the king, as Li, after thanking the royal personage profusely, started out to try his new fins; "not so fast, my friend. Before you depart, perhaps I'd better give you a little friendly advice, else your new powers are likely to land you on the hook of some lucky fisherman, and you will find yourself served up as a prize of the pond."

"I will gladly listen to your lordly counsel, for the words of the Most High to his lowly slave are like pearls before sea slugs. However, as I was once a man myself I think I understand the simple tricks they use to catch us fish, and I am therefore in position to avoid trouble."

"Don't be so sure about it. 'A hungry carp often falls into danger,' as one of our sages so wisely remarked. There are two cautions I would impress upon you. One is, never, never, eat a dangling worm; no matter how tempting it looks there are sure to be horrible hooks inside. Secondly, always swim like lightning if you see a net, but in the opposite direction. Now, I will have you served your first meal out of the royal pantry, but after that, you must hunt for yourself, like every other self-respecting citizen of the watery world."

After Li had been fed with several slugs, followed by a juicy worm for dessert, and after again thanking the king and the king's nephew for their kindness, he started forth to test his tail and fins. It was no easy matter, at first, to move them properly. A single flirt of the tail, no more vigorous than those he had been used to giving with his legs, would send him whirling around and around in the water, for all the world like a living top; and when he wriggled his fins, ever so slightly, as he thought, he found himself sprawling on his back in a most ridiculous fashion for a dignified member of fishkind. It took several hours of constant practice to get the proper stroke, and then he found he could move about without being conscious of any effort. It was the easiest thing he had ever done in his life; and oh! the water was so cool and delightful! "Would that I might enjoy that endless life the poets write of!" he murmured blissfully.

Many hours passed by until at last Li was compelled to admit that, although he was not tired, he was certainly hungry. How to get something to eat? Oh! why had he not asked the friendly nephew a few simple questions? How easily his lordship might have told him the way to get a good breakfast! But alas! without such advice, it would be a whale's task to accomplish it. Hither and thither he swam, into the deep still water, and along the muddy shore; down, down to the pebbly bottom—always looking, looking for a tempting worm. He dived into the weeds and rushes, poked his nose among the lily pads. All for nothing! No fly or worm of any kind to gladden his eager eyes! Another hour passed slowly away, and all the time his hunger was growing greater and greater. Would the fish god, the mighty dragon, not grant him even one little morsel to satisfy his aching stomach, especially since, now that he was a fish, he had no way of tightening up his belt, as hungry soldiers do when they are on a forced march?

Just as Li was beginning to think he could not wriggle his tail an instant longer, and that soon, very soon, he would feel himself slipping, slipping, slipping down to the bottom of the pond to die—at that very moment, chancing to look up, he saw, oh joy! a delicious red worm dangling a few inches above his nose. The sight gave new strength to his weary fins and tail. Another minute, and he would have had the delicate morsel in his mouth, when alas! he chanced to recall the advice given him the day before by great King Carp. "No matter how tempting it looks, there are sure to be horrible hooks inside." For an instant Li hesitated. The worm floated a trifle nearer to his half-open mouth. How tempting! After all, what was a hook to a fish when he was dying? Why be a coward? Perhaps this worm was an exception to the rule, or perhaps, perhaps any thing—really a fish in such a plight as Mr. Li could not be expected to follow advice—even the advice of a real KING.

Pop! He had it in his mouth. Oh, soft morsel, worthy of a king's desire! Now he could laugh at words of wisdom, and eat whatever came before his eye. But ugh! What was that strange feeling that—Ouch! it was the fatal hook!

With one frantic jerk, and a hundred twists and turns, poor Li sought to pull away from the cruel barb that stuck so fast in the roof of his mouth. It was now too late to wish he had kept away from temptation. Better far to have starved at the bottom of the cool pond than to be jerked out by some miserable fisherman to the light and sunshine of the busy world. Nearer and nearer he approached the surface. The more he struggled the sharper grew the cruel barb. Then, with one final splash, he found himself dangling in mid-air, swinging helplessly at the end of a long line. With a chunk he fell into a flat-bottomed boat, directly on top of several smaller fish.

"Ah, a carp!" shouted a well-known voice gleefully; "the biggest fish I've caught these three moons. What good luck!"

It was the voice of old Zhang, the fisherman, who had been supplying Mr. Li's table ever since that official's arrival in the village of Everlasting Happiness. Only a word of explanation, and he, Li, would be free once more to swim about where he willed. And then there should be no more barbs for him. An escaped fish fears the hook.

"I say, Zhang," he began, gasping for breath, "really now, you must chuck me overboard at once, for, don't you see, I am Mr. Li, your old master. Come, hurry up about it. I'll excuse you this time for your mistake, for, of course, you had no way of knowing. Quick!"

But Zhang, with a savage jerk, pulled the hook from Li's mouth, and looked idly towards the pile of glistening fish, gloating over his catch, and wondering how much money he could demand for it. He had heard nothing of Mr. Li's remarks, for Zhang had been deaf since childhood.

"Quick, quick, I am dying for air," moaned poor Li, and then, with a groan, he remembered the fisherman's affliction.

By this time they had arrived at the shore, and Li, in company with his fellow victims, found himself suddenly thrown into a wicker basket. Oh, the horrors of that journey on land! Only a tiny bit of water remained in the closely-woven thing. It was all he could do to breathe.

Joy of joys! At the door of his own house he saw his good friend Xing just coming out. "Hey, Xing," he shouted, at the top of his voice, "help, help! This son of a turtle wants to murder me. He has me in here with these fish, and doesn't seem to know that I am Li, his master. Kindly order him to take me to the lake and throw me in, for it's cool there and I like the water life much better than that on land."

Li paused to hear Xing's reply, but there came not a single word.

"I beg your honor to have a look at my catch," said old Zhang to Xing. "Here is the finest fish of the season. I have brought him here so that you and my honored master, Mr. Li, may have a treat. Carp is his favorite delicacy."

"Very kind of you, my good Zhang, I'm sure, but I fear poor Mr. Li will not eat fish for some time. He has a bad attack of fever."

"There's where you're wrong," shouted Li, from his basket, flopping about with all his might, to attract attention, "I'm going to die of a chill. Can't you recognize your old friend? Help me out of this trouble and you may have all my money for your pains."

"Hey, what's that!" questioned Xing, attracted, as usual, by the word money. "Shades of Confucius! It sounds as if the carp were talking."

"What, a talking fish," laughed Zhang. "Why, master, I've lived nigh on to sixty year, and such a fish has never come under my sight. There are talking birds and talking beasts for that matter; but talking fish, who ever heard of such a wonder? No, I think your ears must have deceived you, but this carp will surely cause talk when I get him into the kitchen. I'm sure the cook has never seen his like. Oh, master! I hope you will be hungry when you sit down to this fish. What a pity Mr. Li couldn't help you to devour it!"

"Help to devour myself, eh?" grumbled poor Li, now almost dead for lack of water. "You must take me for a cannibal, or some other sort of savage."

Old Zhang had now gone around the house to the servants' quarters, and, after calling out the cook, held up poor Li by the tail for the chef to inspect.

With a mighty jerk Li tore himself away and fell at the feet of his faithful cook. "Save me, save me!" he cried out in despair; "this miserable Zhang is deaf and doesn't know that I am Mr. Li, his master. My fish voice is not strong enough for his hearing. Only take me back to the pond and set me free. You shall have a pension for life, wear good clothes and eat good food, all the rest of your days. Only hear me and obey! Listen, my dear cook, listen!"

"The thing seems to be talking," muttered the cook, "but such wonders cannot be. Only ignorant old women or foreigners would believe that a fish could talk." And seizing his former master by the tail, he swung him on to a table, picked up a knife, and began to whet it on a stone.

"Oh, oh!" screamed Li, "you will stick a knife into me! You will scrape off my beautiful shiny scales! You will whack off my lovely new fins! You will murder your old master!"

"Well, you won't talk much longer," growled the cook, "I'll show you a trick or two with the blade."

So saying, with a gigantic thrust, he plunged the knife deep into the body of the trembling victim.

With a shrill cry of horror and despair, Mr. Li awoke from the deep sleep into which he had fallen. His fever was gone, but he found himself trembling with fear at thought of the terrible death that had come to him in dreamland.

"Thanks be to Buddha, I am not a fish!" he cried out joyfully; "and now I shall be well enough to enjoy the feast to which Mr. Xing has bidden guests for tomorrow. But alas, now that I can eat the old fisherman's prize carp, it has changed back into myself."

> "If only the good of our dreams came true,
> I shouldn't mind dreaming the whole day through."

BAMBOO AND THE TURTLE

PARTY of visitors had been seeing the sights at Xi Ling. They had just passed down the Holy Way between the huge stone animals when Bamboo, a little boy of twelve, son of a keeper, rushed out from his father's house to see the mandarins go by. Such a parade of great men he had never seen before, even on the feast days. There were ten sedan chairs, with bearers dressed in flaming colors, ten long-handled, red umbrellas, each carried far in front of its proud owner, and a long line of horsemen.

When this festive procession had filed past, Bamboo was almost ready to cry because he could not run after the sightseers as they went from temple to temple and from tomb to tomb. But, alas! his father had ordered him never to follow tourists. "If you do, they will take you for a beggar, Bamboo," he had said shrewdly, "and if you're a beggar, then your daddy's one too. Now they don't want any beggars around the royal tombs." So Bamboo had never known the pleasure of pursuing the rich. Many times he had turned back to the little mud house, almost broken-hearted at seeing his playmates running, full of glee, after the great men's chairs.

On the day when this story opens, just as the last horseman had passed out of sight among the cedars, Bamboo chanced to look up toward one of the smaller temple buildings of which his father was the keeper. It was the house through which the visitors had just been shown. Could his eyes be deceiving him? No, the great iron doors had been forgotten in the hurry of the moment, and there they stood wide open, as if inviting him to enter.

In great excitement he scurried toward the temple. How often he had pressed his head against the bars and looked into the dark room, wishing and hoping that some day he might go in. And yet, not once had he been granted this favor. Almost every day since babyhood he had gazed at the high stone shaft, or tablet, covered with Chinese writing, that stood in the center of the lofty room, reaching almost to the roof. But with still greater surprise his eyes had feasted on the giant turtle underneath, on whose back the column rested. There are many such tablets to be seen in China, many such turtles patiently bearing their loads of stone, but this was the only sight of the kind that Bamboo had seen. He had never been outside the Xi Ling forest, and, of course, knew very little of the great world beyond.

It is no wonder then that the turtle and the tablet had always astonished him. He had asked his father to explain the mystery. "Why do they have a turtle? Why not a lion or an elephant?" For he had seen stone figures of these animals in the park and had thought them much better able than his friend, the turtle, to carry loads on their backs. "Why it's just the custom," his father had replied—the answer always given when Bamboo asked a question, "just the custom." The boy had tried to imagine it all for himself, but had never been quite sure that he was right, and now, joy of all joys, he was about to enter the very turtle-room itself. Surely, once inside, he could find some answer to this puzzle of his childhood.

Breathless, he dashed through the doorway, fearing every minute that someone would notice the open gates and close them before he could enter. Just in front of the giant turtle he fell in a little heap on the floor, which was covered inch-deep with dust. His face was streaked, his clothes were a sight to behold; but Bamboo cared nothing for such trifles. He lay there for a few moments, not daring to move. Then, hearing a noise outside, he crawled under the ugly stone beast and crouched in his narrow hiding-place, as still as a mouse.

"There, there!" said a deep voice. "See what you are doing, stirring up such a dust! Why, you will strangle me if you are not careful."

It was the turtle speaking, and yet Bamboo's father had often told him that it was not alive. The boy lay trembling for a minute, too much frightened to get up and run.

"No use in shaking so, my lad," the voice continued, a little more kindly. "I suppose all boys are alike—good for nothing but kicking up a dust." He finished this sentence with a hoarse chuckle, and the boy, seeing that he was laughing, looked up with wonder at the strange creature.

"I meant no harm in coming," said the child finally. "I only wanted to look at you more closely."

"Oh, that was it, hey? Well, that is strange. All the others come and stare at the tablet on my back. Sometimes they read aloud the nonsense written there about dead emperors and their titles, but they never so much as look at me, at me whose father was one of the great four who made the world."

Bamboo's eyes shone with wonder. "What! your father helped make the world?" he gasped.

"Well, not my father exactly, but one of my grandfathers, and it amounts to the same thing, doesn't it. But, hark! I hear a voice. The keeper is coming back. Run up and close those doors, so he won't notice that they have not been locked. Then you may hide in the corner there until he has passed. I have something more to tell you."

Bamboo did as he was told. It took all his strength to swing the heavy doors into place. He felt very important to think that he was doing something for the grandson of a maker of the world, and it would have broken his heart if this visit had been ended just as it was beginning.

Sure enough, his father and the other keepers passed on, never dreaming that the heavy locks were not fastened as usual. They were talking about the great men who had just gone. They seemed very happy and were jingling some coins in their hands.

"Now, my boy," said the stone turtle when the sound of voices had died away and Bamboo had come out from his corner, "maybe you think I'm proud of my job. Here I've been holding up this chunk for a hundred years, I who am fond of travel. During all this time night and day, I have been trying to think of some way to give up my position. Perhaps it's honorable, but, you may well imagine, it's not very pleasant."

"I should think you would have the backache," ventured Bamboo timidly.

"Backache! well, I think so; back, neck, legs, eyes, everything I have is aching, aching for freedom. But, you see, even if I had kicked up my heels and overthrown this monument, I had no way of getting through those iron bars," and he nodded toward the gate.

"Yes, I understand," agreed Bamboo, beginning to feel sorry for his old friend.

"But, now that you are here, I have a plan, and a good one it is, too, I think. The watchmen have forgotten to lock the gate. What is to prevent my getting my freedom this very night? You open the gate, I walk out, and no one the wiser."

"But my father will lose his head if they find that he has failed to do his duty and you have escaped."

"Oh, no; not at all. You can slip his keys to-night, lock the gates after I am gone, and no one will know just what has happened. Why it will make this building famous. It won't hurt your father, but will do him good. So many travelers will be anxious to see the spot from which I vanished. I am too heavy for a thief to carry off, and they will be sure that it is another miracle of the gods. Oh, I shall have a good time out in the big world."

Just here Bamboo began to cry.

"Now what is the silly boy blubbering about?" sneered the turtle. "Is he nothing but a cry-baby?"

"No, but I don't want you to go."

"Don't want me to go, eh? Just like all the others. You're a fine fellow! What reason have you for wanting to see me weighed down here all the rest of my life with a mountain on my back? Why, I thought you were sorry for me, and it turns out that you are as mean as anybody else."

"It is so lonely here, and I have no playmates. You are the only friend I have."

The tortoise laughed loudly. "Ho, ho! so it's because I make you a good playmate, eh? Now, if that's your reason, that's another story altogether. What do you say to going with me then? I, too, need a friend, and if you help me to escape, why, you are the very friend for me."

"But how shall you get the tablet off your back?" questioned Bamboo doubtfully. "It's very heavy."

"That's easy, just walk out of the door. The tablet is too tall to go through. It will slide off and sit on the floor instead of on my shell."

Bamboo, wild with delight at the thought of going on a journey with the turtle, promised to obey the other's commands. After supper, when all were asleep in the little house of the keeper, he slipped from his bed, took down the heavy key from its peg, and ran pell-mell to the temple.

"Well, you didn't forget me, did you?" asked the turtle when Bamboo swung the iron gates open.

"Oh, no, I would not break a promise. Are you ready?"

"Yes, quite ready." So saying, the turtle took a step. The tablet swayed backward and forward, but did not fall. On walked the turtle until finally he stuck his ugly head through the doorway. "Oh, how good it looks outside," he said. "How pleasant the fresh air feels! Is that the moon rising over yonder? It's the first time I've seen it for an age. My word! just look at the trees! How they have grown since they set that tombstone on my back! There's a regular forest outside now."

Bamboo was delighted when he saw the turtle's glee at escaping. "Be careful," he cried, "not to let the tablet fall hard enough to break it."

Even as he spoke, the awkward beast waddled through the door. The upper end of the monument struck against the wall, toppled off, and fell with a great crash to the floor. Bamboo shivered with fear. Would his father come and find out what had happened?

"Don't be afraid, my boy. No one will come at this hour of the night to spy on us."

Bamboo quickly locked the gates, ran back to the house, and hung the key on its peg. He took a long look at his sleeping parents, and then returned to his friend. After all, he would not be gone long and his father would surely forgive him.

Soon the comrades were walking down the broad road, very slowly, for the tortoise is not swift of foot and Bamboo's legs were none too long.

"Where are you going?" said the boy at last, after he had begun to feel more at home with the turtle.

"Going? Where should you think I would want to go after my century in prison? Why, back to the first home of my father, back to the very spot where the great god, P'anku, and his three helpers hewed out the world."

"And is it far?" faltered the boy, beginning to feel just the least bit tired.

"At this rate, yes, but, bless my life, you didn't think we could travel all the way at this snail's pace, I hope. Jump on my back, and I'll show you how to go. Before morning we shall be at the end of the world, or rather, the beginning."

"Where is the beginning of the world?" asked Bamboo. "I have never studied geography."

"We must cross China, then Tibet, and at last in the mountains just beyond we shall reach the spot which P'anku made the center of his labor."

At that moment Bamboo felt himself being lifted from the ground. At first he thought he would slip off the turtle's rounded shell, and he cried out in fright.

"Never fear," said his friend. "Only sit quietly, and there will be no danger."

They had now risen far into the air, and Bamboo could look down over the great forest of Xi Ling all bathed in moonlight. There were the broad white roads leading up to the royal tombs, the beautiful temples, the buildings where oxen and sheep were prepared for sacrifice, the lofty towers, and the high tree-covered hills under which the emperors were buried. Until that night Bamboo had not known the size of this royal graveyard. Could it be that the turtle would carry him beyond the forest? Even as he asked himself this question he saw that they had reached a mountain, and the turtle was ascending higher, still higher, to cross the mighty wall of stone.

Bamboo grew dizzy as the turtle rose farther into the sky. He felt as he sometimes did when he played whirling games with his little friends, and got so dizzy that he tumbled over upon the ground. However, this time he knew that he must keep his head and not fall, for it must have been almost a mile to the ground below him. At last they had passed over the mountain and were flying above a great plain. Far below Bamboo could see sleeping villages and little streams of water that looked like silver in the moonlight. Now, directly beneath them was a city. A few feeble lights could be seen in the dark narrow streets, and Bamboo thought he could hear the faint cries of peddlers crying their midnight wares.

"That's the capital of Shanshi just below us," said the turtle, breaking his long silence. "It is almost two hundred miles from here to your father's house, and we have taken less than half an hour. Beyond that is the Province of the Western Valleys. In one hour we shall be above Tibet."

On they whizzed at lightning speed. If it had not been hot summer time Bamboo would have been almost frozen. As it was, his hands and feet were cold and stiff.

The turtle, as if knowing how chilly he was, flew nearer to the ground where it was warmer. How pleasant for Bamboo! He was so tired that he could keep his eyes open no longer and he was soon soaring in the land of dreams.

When he woke up it was morning. He was lying on the ground in a wild, rocky region. Not far away burned a great wood fire, and the turtle was watching some food that was cooking in a pot.

"Ho, ho, my lad! so you have at last woken up after your long ride. You see we are a little early. No matter if the dragon does think he can fly faster, I beat him, didn't I? Why, even the phoenix laughs at me and says I am slow, but the phoenix has not come yet either. Yes, I have clearly broken the record for speed, and I had a load to carry too, which neither of the others had, I am sure."

"Where are we?" questioned Bamboo.

"In the land of the beginning," said the other wisely. "We flew over Tibet, and then went northwest for two hours. If you haven't studied geography you won't know the name of the country. But, here we are, and that is enough, isn't it, enough for anyone? And today is the yearly feast-day in honor of the making of the world. It was very fortunate for me that the gates were left open yesterday. I am afraid my old friends, the dragon and the phoenix, have almost forgotten what I look like. It is so long since they saw me. Lucky beasts they are, not to be loaded down under an emperor's tablet. Hello! I hear the dragon coming now, if I am not mistaken. Yes, here he is. How glad I am to see him!"

Bamboo heard a great noise like the whir of enormous wings, and then, looking up, saw a huge dragon just in front of him. He knew it was a dragon from the pictures he had seen and the carvings in the temples.

The dragon and the turtle had no sooner greeted each other, both very happy at the meeting, than they were joined by a bizarre-looking bird, unlike any that Bamboo had ever seen, but which he knew was the phoenix. This phoenix looked somewhat like a wild swan, but it had the bill of a cock, the neck of a snake, the tail of a fish and the stripes of a dragon. Its feathers were of five colors.

When the three friends had chatted merrily for a few minutes, the turtle told them how Bamboo had helped him to escape from the temple.

"A clever boy," said the dragon, patting Bamboo gently on the back.

"Yes, yes, a clever boy indeed," echoed the phoenix.

"Ah," sighed the turtle, "if only the good god, P'anku, were here, shouldn't we be happy! But, I fear he will never come to this meeting-place. No doubt he is off in some distant spot, cutting out another world. If I could only see him once more, I feel that I should die in peace."

"Just listen!" laughed the dragon. "As if one of us could die! Why, you talk like a mere mortal."

All day long the three friends chatted, feasted, and had a good time looking around at the places where they had lived so happily when P'anku had been cutting out the world. They were good to Bamboo also and showed him many wonderful things of which he had never dreamed.

"You are not half so mean-looking and so fierce as they paint you on the flags," said Bamboo in a friendly voice to the dragon just as they were about to separate.

The three friends laughed heartily.

"Oh, no, he's a very decent sort of fellow, even if he is covered with fish-scales," joked the phoenix.

Just before they bade each other goodbye, the phoenix gave Bamboo a long scarlet tail-feather for a keepsake, and the dragon gave him a large scale which turned to gold as soon as the boy took it into his hand.

"Ah," sighed the turtle, "if only the good god, P'anku, were here."

"Come, come, we must hurry," said the turtle. "I am afraid your father will think you are lost." So Bamboo, after having spent the happiest day of his life, mounted the turtle's back, and they rose once more above the clouds. Back they flew even faster than they had come. Bamboo had so many things to talk about that he did not once think of going to sleep, for he had really seen the dragon and the phoenix, and if he never were to see anything else in his life, he would always be happy.

Suddenly the turtle stopped short in his swift flight, and Bamboo felt himself slipping. Too late he screamed for help, too late he tried to save himself. Down, down from that dizzy height he tumbled, turning, twisting, thinking of the awful death that was surely coming. Swish! he shot through the tree tops trying vainly to clutch the friendly branches. Then with a loud scream he struck the ground, and his long journey was ended.

"Come out from under that turtle, boy! What are you doing inside the temple in the dirt? Don't you know this is not the proper place for you?"

Bamboo rubbed his eyes. Though only half awake, he knew it was his father's voice.

"But didn't it kill me?" he said as his father pulled him out by the heel from under the great stone turtle.

"What killed you, foolish boy? What can you be talking about? But I'll half-kill you if you don't hurry out of this and come to your supper. Really I believe you are getting too lazy to eat. The idea of sleeping the whole afternoon under that turtle's belly!"

Bamboo, not yet fully awake, stumbled out of the tablet room, and his father locked the iron doors.

THE MAD GOOSE AND THE TIGER FOREST

 ULIN was a little slave girl. She had been sold by her father when she was scarcely more than a baby, and had lived for five years with a number of other children in a wretched houseboat. Her cruel master treated her very badly. He made her go out upon the street, with the other girls he had bought, to beg for a living. This kind of life was especially hard for Hulin. She longed to play in the fields, above which the huge kites were sailing in the air like giant birds. She liked to see the crows and magpies flying hither and thither. It was great fun to watch them build their stick nests in the tall poplars. But if her master ever caught her idling her time away in this manner he beat her most cruelly and gave her nothing to eat for a whole day. In fact he was so wicked and cruel that all the children called him Black Heart.

Early one morning when Hulin was feeling very sad about the way she was treated, she resolved to run away, but, alas! she had not gone more than a hundred yards from the houseboat when she saw Black Heart following her. He caught her, scolded her most dreadfully, and gave her such a beating that she felt too faint to stir.

For several hours she lay on the ground without moving a muscle, moaning as if her heart would break. "Ah! if only someone would save me!" she thought, "how good I would be all the rest of my days!"

Now, not far from the river there lived an old man in a tumble-down shanty. The only companion he had was a goose that watched the gate for him at night and screamed out loudly if any stranger dared to prowl about the place. Hulin and this goose were close friends, and the slave girl often stopped to chat with the wise fowl as she was passing the old man's cottage. In this way she had learned that the bird's owner was a miser who kept a great deal of money hidden in his yard. Chang, the goose, had an unusually long neck, and was thus able to pry into most of his master's affairs. As the fowl had no member of his own family to talk with, he told all he knew to Hulin.

On the very morning when Black Heart gave Hulin a beating for trying to run away, Chang made a startling discovery. His lord and master was not really an old miser, but a young man in disguise. Chang, feeling hungry, had slipped into the house at daybreak to see if any scraps had been left from the last evening's meal. The bedroom door had blown open in the night, and there lay a young man sound asleep, instead of the graybeard whom the gander called his master. Then, before his very eyes, the youth changed suddenly into his former shape and was an old man again.

In his excitement, forgetting all about his empty stomach, the terror-stricken goose rushed out into the yard to think over the mystery, but the longer he puzzled, the more strange it all seemed. Then he thought of Hulin, and wished that she would come by, that he might ask her opinion. He had a high regard for the slave girl's knowledge and believed that she would understand fully what had taken place.

Chang went to the gate. As usual, it was locked, and there was nothing for him to do but wait for his master to rise. Two hours later the miser walked out into the yard. He seemed in good spirits, and he gave Chang more to eat than usual. After taking his morning smoke on the street in front of the house, he strolled around it leaving the front gate ajar.

This was precisely what the gander had been expecting. Slipping quietly into the road, he turned towards the river where he could see the houseboats lined up at the wharf. On the sand nearby lay a well-known form.

"Hulin," he called as he drew near, "wake up, for I have something to tell you."

"I am not asleep," she answered, turning her tear-stained face towards her friend.

"Why, what's the matter? You've been crying again. Has old Black Heart been beating you?"

"Hush! he's taking a nap in the boat. Don't let him hear you."

"It's not likely he would understand goose-talk if he did," replied Chang, smiling. "However, I suppose it's always best to be on the safe side, so I'll whisper what I have to say."

Putting his bill close to her ear, he told Hulin of his recent discovery, and ended by asking her to tell him what it all meant.

The child forgot her own misery at hearing his wonderful story. "Are you quite sure there was not some friend of the miser's spending the night with him?" she asked gravely.

"Yes, yes, perfectly sure, for he has no friends," replied the gander. "Besides, I was in the house just before he locked up for the night, and I saw neither hair nor hide of any other person."

"Then he must be a fairy in disguise!" announced Hulin wisely.

"A fairy! what's that?" questioned Chang, more and more excited.

"Why, you old goose, don't you know what a fairy is?" And Hulin laughed outright. By this time she had forgotten her own troubles and was becoming more and more amused at what she had heard. "Hark!" she said in a low tone, and speaking very slowly, "a fairy is—" Here she lowered her voice to a whisper.

The gander nodded violently as she went on with her explanation, and when she had finished, was speechless with amazement, for a few moments. "Well," he said finally, "if my master is that kind of man, suppose you slip away quietly and come with me, for, if a fairy is what you say he is, he can save you from all your troubles and make me happy for the rest of my days."

"I wonder if I dare?" she answered, looking around fearfully towards the houseboat, from the open scuttle of which came the sound of deep snoring.

"Yes, yes, of course!" coaxed Chang. "He gave you such a beating that he won't be afraid of your taking to your heels again very soon."

Putting his bill close to her ear, he told Hulin of his recent discovery.

Hurriedly they went to the miser's compound. Hulin's heart was beating fast as she tried to decide what to say when she should actually stand before the fairy. The gate was still partly open and the two friends entered boldly.

"Come this way," said Chang. "He must be in the backyard digging in his garden."

But when they reached the vegetable patch there was no one to be seen.

"This is very strange," whispered the gander. "I don't understand it, for I have never known him to grow tired of work so early. Surely he cannot have gone in to rest."

Led by her friend, Hulin entered the house on tiptoe. The door of the miser's bedroom stood wide open, and they saw that there was no one either in that room or any other room of the miserable cottage.

"Come! let's see what kind of bed he sleeps on," said Hulin, filled with curiosity. "I have never been in a fairy's room. It must be different from other people's rooms."

"No, no! just a plain brick bed, like all the rest," answered Chang, as they crossed the threshold.

"Does he have a fire in cold weather?" asked Hulin, stooping to examine the small fire hole in the bricks.

"Oh, yes, a hot fire every night, and even in spring when other people have stopped having fires, the brick bed is hot every night."

"Well, that's rather strange for a miser, don't you think?" said the girl. "It costs more to keep a fire going than it does to feed a man."

"Yes, that's true," agreed Chang, pruning his feathers. "I hadn't thought of that. It is strange, very. Hulin, you're a wise child. Where did you learn so much?"

At that moment the gander turned pale at hearing the gate slam loudly and the bar thrown into place.

"Good gracious! what ever shall we do?" asked Hulin. "What will he say if he finds us here?"

"No telling," said the other, trembling, "but, my dear little friend, we are certainly caught, for we can't get away without his seeing us."

"Yes, and I've already had one beating today! And such a hard one that I don't believe I could live through another," sighed the child, as the tears began to flow.

"There, there, little girl, don't worry! Let's hide in this dark corner behind the baskets," suggested the gander, just as the master's step was heard at the front door.

Soon the frightened companions were crouching on the ground, trying to hide. Much to their relief, however, the miser did not go into his bedroom, and they soon heard him hard at work in the garden. All that day the two remained in their hiding place, afraid to show themselves outside the door.

"I can't imagine what he would say if he found out that his watch-goose had brought a stranger into the house," said Chang.

"Perhaps he would think we were trying to steal some of the money he has hidden away," she answered, laughing, for as Hulin became used to her cramped quarters she grew less frightened. At any rate she was not nearly so much afraid of the miser as she had thought she was. "Besides," she reflected, "he can't be so bad as old Black Heart."

Thus the day wore on and darkness fell over the land. By this time girl and goose were fast asleep in one corner of the miser's room and knew nothing more of what was happening.

When the first light of a new day filtered through the paper-covered window above the miser's bed, Hulin awoke with a start, and at first she could not think where she was. Chang was staring at her with wide-open frightened eyes that seemed to be asking, "What can it all mean? It is more than my goose brain can think out."

For on the bed, instead of the miser, there lay a young man whose hair was a black as a raven's wing. A faint smile lightened up his handsome face, as if he was enjoying some delightful dream. A cry of wonder escaped Hulin's lips before she could hold it back. The sleeper's eyes opened instantly and were fixed upon her. The girl was so frightened that she could not move, and the gander trembled violently as he saw the change that had come over his master.

The young man was even more surprised than his guests, and for two minutes he was speechless. "What does this mean?" he asked, finally, looking at Chang. "What are you doing in my bedroom and who is this child who seems so frightened?"

"Forgive me, kind sir, but what have you done to my master?" asked the gander, giving question for question.

"Am I not your master, you mad creature?" said the man, laughing. "You are more stupid than ever this morning."

"My master was old and ugly, but you are still young and handsome," replied Chang in a tone of flattery.

"What," shouted the other, "you say I am still young?"

"Why, yes. Ask Hulin, if you don't believe me."

The man turned towards the little girl.

"Yes, indeed you are, sir," she replied in answer to his look. "Never have I seen a man so beautiful."

"At last! at last!" he cried, laughing joyfully, "I am free, free, free from all my troubles, but how it has come about is more than I can say!"

For a few minutes he stood in a deep study, snapping his long fingers as if trying to solve some hard problem. At last a smile lighted up his face. "Chang," he asked, "what was it you called your guest when you spoke of her a minute ago?"

"I am Hulin," said the child simply, "Hulin, the slave girl."

He clapped his hands. "That's right! That's right!" he cried. "I see it all now; it is as plain as day." Then, noticing the look of wonder on her face, "It is to you that I owe my freedom from a wicked fairy, and if you like, I'll tell you the story of my misfortune."

"Pray do, kind sir," she replied eagerly. "I told Chang that you were a fairy, and I should like to know if I was right."

"Well, you see," he began, "my father is a rich man who lives in a distant county. When I was a boy he gave me everything I wished. I was so humored and spoiled from earliest childhood that at last I began to think there was nothing at all in the world I could not have for the asking, and nothing that I must not do if I wished to.

"My teacher often scolded me for having such notions. He told me there was a proverb: 'Men die for gain, birds perish to get food.' He thought such men were very foolish. He told me that money would go a long way towards making a man happy, but he always ended by saying that the gods were more powerful than men. He said I must always be careful not to make the evil spirits angry. Sometimes I laughed in his face, telling him that I was rich and could buy the favor of gods and fairies. The good man would shake his head, saying, 'Take care, my boy, or you will be sorry for these rash speeches.'"

"One day, after he had been giving me a long lecture of this sort, we were walking in the garden of my father's compound. I was even more daring than usual and told him that I cared nothing for the rules other people followed. 'You say,' said I, 'that this well here in my father's yard is ruled by a spirit, and that if I were to anger him by jumping over it, he would be vexed and give me trouble.' 'Yes,' said he, 'that is exactly what I said, and I repeat it. Beware, young man, beware of idle boasting and of breaking the law.' 'What do I care for a spirit that lives on my father's land?' I answered with a sneer. 'I don't believe there is a spirit in this well. If there is, it is only another of my father's slaves.'

"So saying, and before my tutor could stop me, I leaped across the mouth of the well. No sooner had I touched the ground than I felt a strange shrinking of my body. My strength left me in the twinkling of an eye, my bones shortened, my skin grew yellow and wrinkled. I looked at my pigtail and found that the hair had suddenly grown thin and white. In every way I had been changed completely into an old man.

"My teacher stared at me in amazement, and when I asked him what it all meant my voice was as shrill as that of early childhood. 'Alas! my dear pupil,' he replied, 'now you will believe what I told you. The spirit of the well is angry at your wicked conduct and has punished you. You have been told a hundred times that it is wrong to leap over a well; yet you did this very thing,' 'But is there nothing that can be done,' I cried; 'is there no way of restoring my lost youth?' He looked at me sadly and shook his head.

"When my father learned of my sad condition he was terribly upset. He did everything that could be done to find some way for me to regain my youth. He had incense burned at a dozen temples and he himself offered up prayers to various gods. I was his only son, and he could not be happy without me. At last, when everything else had been done, my worthy teacher thought of asking a fortune-teller who had become famous in the city. After inquiring about everything that had led up to my sad plight, the wise man said that the spirit of the well, as a punishment, had changed me into a miser. He said that only when I was sleeping would I be in my natural state, and even then if anyone chanced to enter my room or catch a glimpse of my face, I would be at once changed back into a graybeard."

"I saw you yesterday morning," shouted the gander. "You were young and handsome, and then before my very eyes you were changed back into an old man!"

"To continue my story," said the young man, "the fortune-teller at last announced that there was only one chance for my recovery and that a very small one. If at any time, while I was in my rightful shape, that is, as you see me now, a mad goose should come in, leading a tiger-forest out of slavery, the charm would be broken, and the evil spirit would no longer have control over me. When the fortune-teller's answer was brought to my father, he gave up hope, and so did I, for no one understood the meaning of such a senseless riddle.

"That night I left my native city, resolved not to disgrace my people any longer by living with them. I came to this place, bought this house with some money my father had given me, and at once began living the life of a miser. Nothing satisfied my greed for money. Everything must be turned into cash. For five years I have been storing away money, and, at the same time, starving myself, body and soul.

"Soon after my arrival here, remembering the fortune-teller's riddle, I decided that I would keep a goose to serve as night watchman instead of a dog. In this way I made a start at working out the riddle."

"But I am not a mad goose," hissed the gander angrily. "If it had not been for me you would still be a wrinkled miser."

"Quite right, dear Chang, quite right," said the young man soothingly; "you were not mad; so I gave you the name Chang, which means mad, and thus made a mad goose of you."

"Oh, I see," said Hulin and Chang together. "How clever!"

"So, you see, I had part of my cure here in my back-yard all the time; but though I thought as hard as I could, I could think of no way of securing that Chang should lead a tiger-forest into my room while I was sleeping. The thing seemed absurd, and I soon gave up trying to study it out. Today by accident it has really come to pass."

"So I am the tiger-forest, am I?" laughed Hulin.

"Yes, indeed, you are, my dear child, a pretty little tiger-forest, for *Hu* means *tiger*, and *lin* is surely good Chinese for a *grove of trees*. Then, too, you told me you were a slave girl. Hence, Chang led you out of slavery."

"Oh, I am so glad!" said Hulin, forgetting her own poverty, "so glad that you don't have to be a horrible old miser any longer."

Just at that moment there was a loud banging on the front gate.

"Who can be knocking in that fashion?" asked the young man in astonishment.

"Alas! it must be Black Heart, my master," said Hulin, beginning to cry.

"Don't be frightened," said the youth, soothingly stroking the child's head. "You have saved me, and I shall certainly do as much for you. If this Mr. Black Heart doesn't agree to a fair proposal he shall have a black eye to remember his visit by."

It did not take long for the grateful young man to buy Hulin's liberty, especially as he of-fered as much for her freedom as her master had expected to get when she was fourteen or fifteen years of age.

When Hulin was told of the bargain she was wild with delight. She bowed low before her new master and then, kneeling, touched her head nine times on the floor. Rising, she cried out, "Oh, how happy I am, for now I shall be yours forever and ever and ever, and good old Chang shall be my playmate."

"Yes, indeed," he assured her, "and when you are a little older I shall make you my wife. At present you will go with me to my father's house and become my little betrothed."

"And I shall never again have to beg for crusts on the street?" she asked him, her eyes full of wonder.

"No! never!" he answered, laughing, "and you need never fear another beating."

THE NODDING TIGER

 UST outside the walls of a Chinese city there lived a young woodcutter named Tang and his old mother, a woman of seventy. They were very poor and had a tiny one-room shanty, built of mud and grass, which they rented from a neighbor. Every day young Tang rose bright and early and went up on the mountain near their house. There he spent the day cutting firewood to sell in the city near by. In the evening he would return home, take the wood to market, sell it, and bring back food for his mother and himself. Now, though these two people were poor, they were very happy, for the young man loved his mother dearly, and the old woman thought there was no one like her son in all the world. Their friends, however, felt sorry for them and said, "What a pity we have no grasshoppers here, so that the Tangs could have some food from heaven!"

One day young Tang got up before daylight and started for the hills, carrying his axe on his shoulder. He bade his mother goodbye, telling her that he would be back early with a heavier load of wood than usual, for the following day would be a holiday and they must eat good food. All day long Widow Tang waited patiently, saying to herself over and over as she went about her simple work, "The good boy, the good boy, how he loves his old mother!"

In the afternoon she began watching for his return—but in vain. The sun was sinking lower and lower in the west, but still he did not come. At last the old woman was frightened. "My poor son!" she muttered. "Something has happened to him." Straining her feeble eyes, she looked along the mountain path. Nothing was to be seen there but a flock of sheep following the shepherd. "Woe is me!" moaned the woman. "My boy! my boy!" She took her crutch from its corner and limped off to a neighbor's house to tell him of her trouble and beg him to go and look for the missing boy.

Now this neighbor was kind-hearted, and willing to help old Mother Tang, for he felt very sorry for her. "There are many wild beasts in the mountains," he said, shaking his head as he walked away with her, thinking to prepare the frightened woman for the worst, "and I fear that your son has been carried off by one of them." Widow Tang gave a scream of horror and sank upon the ground. Her friend walked slowly up the mountain path, looking carefully for signs of a struggle. At last when he had gone halfway up the slope he came to a little pile of torn clothing spattered with blood. The woodman's axe was lying by the side of the path, also his carrying pole and some rope. There could be no mistake: after making a brave fight, the poor youth had been carried off by a tiger.

Gathering up the torn garments, the man went sadly down the hill. He dreaded seeing the poor mother and telling her that her only boy was indeed gone forever. At the foot of the mountain he found her still lying on the ground. When she looked up and saw what he was carrying, with a cry of despair she fainted away. She did not need to be told what had happened.

Friends bore her into the little house and gave her food, but they could not comfort her. "Alas!" she cried, "of what use is it to live? He was my only boy. Who will take care of me in my old age? Why have the gods treated me in this cruel way?"

She wept, tore her hair, and beat her chest, until people said she had gone mad. The longer she mourned, the more violent she became.

The next day, however, much to the surprise of her neighbors, she set out for the city, making her way along slowly by means of her crutch. It was a pitiful sight to see her, so old, so feeble, and so lonely. Everyone was sorry for her and pointed her out, saying, "See! the poor old soul has no one to help her!"

In the city she asked her way to the public hall. When she found the place she knelt at the front gate, calling out loudly and telling of her ill-fortune. Just at this moment the mandarin, or city judge, walked into the court room to try any cases which might be brought before him. He heard the old woman weeping and wailing outside, and bade one of the servants let her enter and tell him of her wrongs.

Now this was just what the Widow Tang had come for. Calming herself, she hobbled into the great hall of trial.

"What is the matter, old woman? Why do you raise such an uproar in front of my *yamen*? Speak up quickly and tell me of your trouble."

"I am old and feeble," she began, "lame and almost blind. I have no money and no way of earning money. I have not one relative now in all the empire. I depended on my only son for a living. Every day he climbed the mountain, for he was a woodcutter, and every evening he came back home, bringing enough money for our food. But yesterday he went and did not return. A mountain tiger carried him off and ate him, and now, alas! there seems to be no help for it—I must die of hunger. My bleeding heart cries out for justice. I have come into this hall today, to beg your worship to see that the slayer of my son is punished. Surely the law says that none may shed blood without giving his own blood in payment."

"But, woman, are you mad?" cried the mandarin, laughing loudly. "Did you not say it was a tiger that killed your son? How can a tiger be brought to justice? Truly, you must have lost your senses."

The judge's questions were of no avail. The Widow Tang kept up her clamor. She would not be turned away until she had gained her purpose. The hall echoed with the noise of her howling. The mandarin could stand it no longer. "Hold! woman," he cried, "stop your shrieking. I will do what you ask. Only go home and wait until I summon you to court. The slayer of your son shall be caught and punished."

The judge was, of course, only trying to get rid of the demented mother, thinking that if she were only once out of his sight, he could give orders not to let her into the hall again. The old woman, however, was too sharp for him. She saw through his plan and became more stubborn than ever.

"No, I cannot go," she answered, "until I have seen you sign the order for that tiger to be caught and brought into this judgment hall."

Now, as the judge was not really a bad man, he decided to humor the old woman in her strange plea. Turning to the assistants in the court room he asked which of them would be willing to go in search of the tiger. One of these men, named Lineng, had been leaning against the wall, half asleep. He had been drinking heavily and so had not heard what had been going on in the room. One of his friends gave him a poke in the ribs just as the judge asked for volunteers.

Thinking the judge had called him by name, he stepped forward, knelt on the floor, saying, "I, Lineng, can go and do the will of your worship."

"Very well, you will do," answered the judge. "Here is your order. Go forth and do your duty." So saying, he handed the warrant to Lineng. "Now, old woman, are you satisfied?" he continued.

"Quite satisfied, your worship," she replied.

"Then go home and wait there until I send for you."

Mumbling a few words of thanks, the unhappy mother left the building.

When Lineng went outside the court room, his friends crowded around him. "Drunken sot!" they laughed; "do you know what you have done?"

Lineng shook his head. "Just a little business for the mandarin, isn't it? Quite easy."

"Call it easy, if you like. What! man, arrest a tiger, a man-eating tiger and bring him to the city! Better go and say goodbye to your father and mother. They will never see you again."

Lineng slept off his drunkenness, and then saw that his friends were right. He had been very foolish. But surely the judge had meant the whole thing only as a joke! No such order had ever been written before! It was plain that the judge had hit on this plan simply to get rid of the wailing old woman. Lineng took the warrant back to the judgment hall and told the mandarin that the tiger could not be found.

But the judge was in no mood for joking. "Can't be found? And why not? You agreed to arrest this tiger. Why is it that today you try to get out of your promise? I can by no means permit this, for I have given my word to satisfy the old woman in her cry for justice."

Lineng knelt and knocked his head on the floor. "I was drunk," he cried, "when I gave my promise. I knew not what you were asking. I can catch a man, but not a tiger. I know nothing of such matters. Still, if you wish it, I can go into the hills and hire hunters to help me."

"Very well, it makes no difference how you catch him, as long as you bring him into court. If you fail in your duty, there is nothing left but to beat you until you succeed. I give you five days."

During the next few days Lineng left no stone unturned in trying to find the guilty tiger. The best hunters in the country were employed. Night and day they searched the hills, hiding in mountain caves, watching and waiting, but finding nothing. It was all very trying for Lineng, since he now feared the heavy hands of the judge more than the claws of the tiger. On the fifth day he had to report his failure. He received a thorough beating, fifty blows on the back. But that was not the worst of it. During the next six weeks, try as he would, he could find no traces of the missing animal. At the end of each five days, he got another beating for his pains. The poor fellow was in despair. Another month of such treatment would lay him on his deathbed. This he knew very well, and yet he had little hope. His friends shook their heads when they saw him. "He is drawing near the wood," they said to each other, meaning that he would soon be in his coffin. "Why don't you flee the country?" they asked him. "Follow the tiger's example. You see he has escaped completely. The judge would make no effort to catch you if you should go across the border into the next province."

Lineng shook his head on hearing this advice. He had no desire to leave his family for ever, and he felt sure of being caught and put to death if he should try to run away.

One day after all the hunters had given up the search in disgust and gone back to their homes in the valley, Lineng entered a mountain temple to pray. The tears rained down his cheeks as he knelt before the great fierce-looking idol. "Alas! I am a dead man!" he moaned between his prayers; "a dead man, for now there is no hope. Would that I had never touched a drop of wine!"

Just then he heard a slight rustling near by. Looking up, he saw a huge tiger standing at the temple gate. But Lineng was no longer afraid of tigers. He knew there was only one way to save himself. "Ah," he said, looking the great cat straight in the eye, "you have come to eat me, have you? Well, I fear you would find my flesh a trifle tough, since I have been beaten with four hundred blows during these six weeks. You are the same fellow that carried off the woodman last month, aren't you? This woodman was an only son, the sole support of an old mother. Now this poor woman has reported you to the mandarin, who, in turn, has had a warrant drawn up for your arrest. I have been sent out to find you and lead you to trial. For some reason or other you have acted the coward, and remained in hiding. This has been the cause of my beating. Now I don't want to suffer any longer as a result of your murder. You must come with me to the city and answer the charge of killing the woodman."

All the time Lineng was speaking, the tiger listened closely. When the man was silent, the animal made no effort to escape, but, on the contrary, seemed willing and ready to be captured. He bent his head forward and let Lineng slip a strong chain over it. Then he followed the man quietly down the mountain, through the crowded streets of the city, into the court room. All along the way there was great excitement. "The man-slaying tiger has been caught," shouted the people. "He is being led to trial."

The crowd followed Lineng into the hall of justice. When the judge walked in, everyone became as quiet as the grave. All were filled with wonder at the strange sight of a tiger being called before a judge.

The great animal did not seem to be afraid of those who were watching so curiously. He sat down in front of the mandarin, for all the world like a huge cat. The judge rapped on the table as a signal that all was ready for the trial.

"Tiger," said he, turning toward the prisoner, "did you eat the woodman whom you are charged with killing?"

The tiger gravely nodded his head.

"Yes, he killed my boy!" screamed the aged mother. "Kill him! Give him the death that he deserves!"

"A life for a life is the law of the land," continued the judge, paying no attention to the forlorn mother, but looking the accused directly in the eye. "Did you not know it? You have robbed a helpless old woman of her only son. There are no relatives to support her. She is crying for vengeance. You must be punished for your crime. The law must be enforced. However, I am not a cruel judge. If you can promise to take the place of this widow's son and support the woman in her old age, I am quite willing to spare you from a disgraceful death. What say you, will you accept my offer?"

The gaping people craned their necks to see what would happen, and once more they were surprised to see the savage beast nod his head in silent agreement.

"Very well, then, you are free to return to your mountain home; only, of course, you must remember your promise."

The tiger gravely nodded his head.

The chains were taken from the tiger's neck, and the great animal walked silently out of the *yamen*, down the street, and through the gate opening towards his beloved mountain cave.

Once more the old woman was very angry. As she hobbled from the room, she cast sour glances at the judge, muttering over and over again, "Who ever heard of a tiger taking the place of a son? A pretty game this is, to catch the brute, and then to set him free." There was nothing for her to do, however, but to return home, for the judge had given strict orders that on no account was she to appear before him again.

Almost broken-hearted she entered her desolate hovel at the foot of the mountain. Her neighbors shook their heads as they saw her. "She cannot live long," they said. "She has the look of death on her wrinkled face. Poor soul! she has nothing to live for, nothing to keep her from starving."

But they were mistaken. Next morning when the old woman went outside to get a breath of fresh air she found a newly killed deer in front of her door. Her tiger-son had begun to keep his promise, for she could see the marks of his claws on the dead animal's body. She took the carcass into the house and dressed it for the market. On the city streets next day she had no trouble in selling the flesh and skin for a handsome sum of money. All had heard of the tiger's first gift, and no one was anxious to drive a close bargain.

Laden with food, the happy woman went home rejoicing, with money enough to keep her for many a day. A week later the tiger came to her door with a roll of cloth and some money in his mouth. He dropped these new gifts at her feet and ran away without even waiting for her thank-you. The Widow Tang now saw that the judge had acted wisely. She stopped grieving for her dead son and began to love in his stead the handsome animal that had come to take his place so willingly.

The tiger grew much attached to his foster-mother and often purred contentedly outside her door, waiting for her to come and stroke his soft fur. He no longer had the old desire to kill. The sight of blood was not nearly so tempting as it had been in his younger days. Year after year he brought the weekly offerings to his mistress until she was as well provided for as any other widow in the country.

At last in the course of nature the good old soul died. Kind friends laid her away in her last resting place at the foot of the great mountain. There was money enough left out of what she had saved to put up a handsome tombstone, on which this story was written just as you have read it here. The faithful tiger mourned long for his dear mistress. He lay on her grave, wailing like a child that had lost its mother. Long he listened for the voice he had loved so well, long he searched the mountain-slopes, returning each night to the empty cottage, but all in vain. She whom he loved was gone for ever.

One night he vanished from the mountain, and from that day to this no one in that province has ever seen him. Some who know this story say that he died of grief in a secret cave which he had long used as a hiding-place. Others add, with a wise shrug of the shoulders, that, like Shanwang, he was taken to the Western Heaven, there to be rewarded for his deeds of virtue and to live as a fairy for ever afterwards.

THE PRINCESS GUANYIN

NCE upon a time in China there lived a certain king who had three daughters. The fairest and best of these was Guanyin, the youngest. The old king was justly proud of this daughter, for of all the women who had ever lived in the palace she was by far the most attractive. It did not take him long, therefore, to decide that she should be the heir to his throne, and her husband ruler of his kingdom. But, strange to say, Guanyin was not pleased at this good fortune. She cared little for the pomp and splendor of court life. She foresaw no pleasure for herself in ruling as a queen, but even feared that in so high a station she might feel out of place and unhappy.

Every day she went to her room to read and study. As a result of this daily labor she soon went far beyond her sisters along the paths of knowledge, and her name was known in the farthest corner of the kingdom as "Guanyin, the wise princess." Besides being very fond of books, Guanyin was thoughtful of her friends. She was careful about her behavior both in public and in private. Her warm heart was open at all times to the cries of those in trouble. She was kind to the poor and suffering. She won the love of the lower classes, and was to them a sort of goddess to whom they could appeal whenever they were hungry and in need. Some people even believed that she was a fairy who had come to earth from her home within the Western Heaven, while others said that once, long years before, she had lived in the world as a prince instead of a princess. However this may be, one thing is certain—Guanyin was pure and good, and well deserved the praises that were showered upon her.

One day the king called this favorite daughter to the royal bedside, for he felt that the hour of death was drawing near. Guanyin kowtowed before her royal father, kneeling and touching her forehead on the floor in sign of deepest reverence. The old man bade her rise and come closer. Taking her hand tenderly in his own, he said, "Daughter, you know well how I love you. Your modesty and virtue, your talent and your love of knowledge, have made you first in my heart. As you know already, I chose you as heir to my kingdom long ago. I promised that your husband should be made ruler in my stead. The time is almost ripe for me to ascend upon the dragon and become a guest on high. It is necessary that you be given at once in marriage."

"But, most exalted father," faltered the princess, "I am not ready to be married."

"Not ready, child! Why, are you not eighteen? Are not the daughters of our nation often wedded long before they reach that age? Because of your desire for learning I have spared you thus far from any thought of a husband, but now we can wait no longer."

"Royal father, hear your child, and do not compel her to give up her dearest pleasures. Let her go into a quiet convent where she may lead a life of study!"

The king sighed deeply at hearing these words. He loved his daughter and did not wish to wound her. "Guanyin," he continued, "do you wish to pass by the green spring of youth, to give up this mighty kingdom? Do you wish to enter the doors of a convent where women say farewell to life and all its pleasures? No! your father will not permit this. It grieves me sorely to disappoint you, but one month from this very day you shall be married. I have chosen for your royal partner a man of many noble parts. You know him by name already, although you have not seen him. Remember that, of the hundred virtues filial conduct is the chief, and that you owe more to me than to all else on earth."

Guanyin turned pale. Trembling, she would have sunk to the floor, but her mother and sisters supported her, and by their tender care brought her back to consciousness.

Every day of the month that followed, Guanyin's relatives begged her to give up what they called her foolish notion. Her sisters had long since given up hope of becoming queen. They were amazed at her stupidity. The very thought of anyone's choosing a convent instead of a throne was to them a sure sign of madness. Over and over again they asked her reason for making so strange a choice. To every question, she shook her head, replying, "A voice from the heavens speaks to me, and I must obey it."

On the eve of the wedding day Guanyin slipped out of the palace, and, after a weary journey, arrived at a convent called, "The Cloister of the White Sparrow." She was dressed as a poor maiden. She said she wished to become a nun. The abbess, not knowing who she was, did not receive her kindly. Indeed, she told Guanyin that they could not receive her into the sisterhood, that the building was full. Finally, after Guanyin had shed many tears, the abbess let her enter, but only as a sort of servant, who might be cast out for the slightest fault.

Now that Guanyin found herself in the life which she had long dreamt of leading, she tried to be satisfied. But the nuns seemed to wish to make her stay among them most miserable. They gave her the hardest tasks to do, and it was seldom that she had a minute to rest. All day long she was busy, carrying water from a well at the foot of the convent hill or gathering wood from a neighboring forest. At night when her back was almost breaking, she was given many extra tasks, enough to have crushed the spirit of any other woman than this brave daughter of a king. Forgetting her grief, and trying to hide the lines of pain that sometimes wrinkled her fair forehead, she tried to make these hard-hearted women love her. In return for their rough words, she spoke to them kindly, and never did she give way to anger.

One day while poor Guanyin was picking up brushwood in the forest she heard a tiger making his way through the bushes. Having no means of defending herself, she breathed a silent prayer to the gods for help, and calmly awaited the coming of the great beast. To her surprise, when the bloodthirsty animal appeared, instead of bounding up to tear her in pieces, he began to make a soft purring noise. He did not try to hurt Guanyin, but rubbed against her in a friendly manner, and let her pat him on the head.

The next day the princess went back to the same spot. There she found no fewer than a dozen savage beasts working under the command of the friendly tiger, gathering wood for her. In a short time enough brush and firewood had been piled up to last the convent for six months. Thus, even the wild animals of the forest were better able to judge of her goodness than the women of the sisterhood.

At another time when Guanyin was toiling up the hill for the twentieth time, carrying two great pails of water on a pole, an enormous dragon faced her in the road. Now, in China, the dragon is sacred, and Guanyin was not at all frightened, for she knew that she had done no wrong.

The animal looked at her for a moment, switched its horrid tail, and shot out fire from its nostrils. Then, dashing the burden from the startled maiden's shoulder, it vanished. Full of fear, Guanyin hurried up the hill to the nunnery. As she drew near the inner court, she was amazed to see in the center of the open space a new building of solid stone. It had sprung up by magic since her last journey down the hill. On going forward, she saw that there were four arched doorways to the fairy house. Above the door facing west was a tablet with these words written on it: "In honor of Guanyin, the faithful princess." Inside was a well of the purest water, while, for drawing this water, there a strange machine, the like of which neither Guanyin nor the nuns had ever seen.

All day long she was busy carrying water.

The sisters knew that this magic well was a monument to Guanyin's goodness. For a few days they treated her much better. "Since the gods have dug a well at our very gate," they said, "this girl will no longer need to bear water from the foot of the hill. For what strange reason, however, did the gods write this beggar's name on the stone?"

Guanyin heard their unkind remarks in silence. She could have explained the meaning of the dragon's gift, but she chose to let her companions remain in ignorance. At last the selfish nuns began to grow careless again, and treated her even worse than before. They could not bear to see the poor girl enjoy a moment's idleness.

"This is a place for work," they told her. "All of us have labored hard to win our present station. You must do likewise." So they robbed her of every chance for study and prayer, and gave her no credit for the magic well.

One night the sisters were awakened from their sleep by strange noises, and soon they heard outside the walls of the compound the blare of a trumpet. A great army had been sent by Guanyin's father to attack the convent, for his spies had at last been able to trace the runaway princess to this holy retreat.

"Oh, who has brought this woe upon us?" exclaimed all the women, looking at each other in great fear. "Who has done this great evil? There is one among us who has sinned most terribly, and now the gods are about to destroy us." They gazed at one another, but no one thought of Guanyin, for they did not believe her of enough importance to attract the anger of heaven, even though she might have done the most shocking of deeds. Then, too, she had been so meek and lowly while in their holy order that they did not once dream of charging her with any crime.

The threatening sounds outside grew louder and louder. All at once a fearful cry arose among the women: "They are about to burn our sacred dwelling." Smoke was rising just beyond the enclosure where the soldiers were kindling a great fire, the heat of which would soon be great enough to make the convent walls crumble into dust.

Suddenly a voice was heard above the tumult of the weeping sisters: "Alas! I am the cause of all this trouble."

The nuns, turning in amazement, saw that it was Guanyin who was speaking. "You?" they exclaimed, astounded.

"Yes, I, for I am indeed the daughter of a king. My father did not wish me to take the vows of this holy order. I fled from the palace. He has sent his army here to burn these buildings and to drag me back a prisoner."

"Then, see what you have brought upon us, miserable girl!" exclaimed the abbess. "See how you have repaid our kindness! Our buildings will be burned above our heads! How wretched you have made us! May heaven's curses rest upon you!"

"No, no!" exclaimed Guanyin, springing up, and trying to keep the abbess from speaking these frightful words. "You have no right to say that, for I am innocent of evil. But, wait! You shall soon see whose prayers the gods will answer, yours or mine!" So saying, she pressed her forehead to the floor, praying the almighty powers to save the convent and the sisters.

Outside the crackling of the greedy flames could already be heard. The fire king would soon destroy every building on that hill-top. Mad with terror, the sisters prepared to leave the compound and give up all their belongings to the cruel flames and still more cruel soldiers. Guanyin alone remained in the room, praying earnestly for help.

Suddenly a soft breeze sprang up from the neighboring forest, dark clouds gathered overhead, and, although it was the dry season a drenching shower descended on the flames. Within five minutes the fire was put out and the convent was saved. Just as the shivering nuns were thanking Guanyin for the divine help she had brought them, two soldiers who had scaled the outer wall of the compound came in and roughly asked for the princess.

The trembling girl, knowing that these men were obeying her father's orders, poured out a prayer to the gods, and straightway made herself known. They dragged her from the presence of the nuns who had just begun to love her. Thus disgraced before her father's army, she was taken to the capital.

The following day, she was led before the old king. The father gazed sadly at his daughter, and then the stern look of a judge hardened his face as he beckoned the guards to bring her forward.

From a neighboring room came the sounds of sweet music. A feast was being served there amid great splendor. The loud laughter of the guests reached the ears of the young girl as she bowed in disgrace before her father's throne. She knew that this feast had been prepared for her, and that her father was willing to give her one more chance.

"Girl," said the king, at last regaining his voice, "in leaving the royal palace on the eve of your wedding day, not only did you insult your father, but your king. For this act you deserve to die. However, because of the excellent record you had made for yourself before you ran away, I have decided to give you one more chance to redeem yourself. Refuse me, and the penalty is death: obey me, and all may yet be well—the kingdom that you spurned is still yours for the asking. All that I require is your marriage to the man whom I have chosen."

"And when, most august King, would you have me decide?" asked Guanyin earnestly.

"This very day, this very hour, this very moment," he answered sternly. "What! would you hesitate between love upon a throne and death? Speak, my daughter, tell me that you love me and will do my bidding!"

It was now all that Guanyin could do to keep from throwing herself at her father's feet and yielding to his wishes, not because he offered her a kingdom, but because she loved him and would gladly have made him happy. But her strong will kept her from relenting. No power on earth could have stayed her from doing what she thought her duty.

"Beloved father," she answered sadly, and her voice was full of tenderness, "it is not a question of my love for you—of that there is no question, for all my life I have shown it in every action. Believe me, if I were free to do your bidding, gladly would I make you happy, but a voice from the gods has spoken, has commanded that I remain a virgin, that I devote my life to deeds of mercy. When heaven itself has commanded, what can even a princess do but listen to that power which rules the earth?"

The old king was far from satisfied with Guanyin's answer. He grew furious, his thin wrinkled skin turned purple as the hot blood rose to his head. "Then you refuse to do my bidding! Take her, men! Give to her the death that is due to a traitor to the king!" As they bore Guanyin away from his presence the white-haired monarch fell, swooning, from his chair.

That night, when Guanyin was put to death, she descended into the lower world of torture. No sooner had she set foot in that dark country of the dead than the vast region of endless punishment suddenly blossomed forth and became like the gardens of Paradise. Pure white lilies sprang up on every side, and the odor of a million flowers filled all the rooms and corridors. King Yama, ruler of the dominion, rushed forth to learn the cause of this wonderful change. No sooner did his eyes rest upon the fair young face of Guanyin than he saw in her the emblem of a purity which deserved no home but heaven.

"Beautiful virgin, doer of many mercies," he began, after addressing her by her title, "I beg you in the name of justice to depart from this bloody kingdom. It is not right that the fairest flower of heaven should enter and shed her fragrance in these halls. Guilt must suffer here, and sin find no reward. Depart thou, then, from my dominion. The peach of immortal life shall be bestowed upon you, and heaven alone shall be your dwelling place."

Thus Guanyin became the Goddess of Mercy; thus she entered into that glad abode, surpassing all earthly kings and queens. And ever since that time, on account of her exceeding goodness, thousands of poor people breathe out to her each year their prayers for mercy. There is no fear in their gaze as they look at her beautiful image, for their eyes are filled with tears of love.

THE TWO JUGGLERS

NE beautiful spring day two men strolled into the public square of a well-known Chinese city. They were plainly dressed and looked like ordinary countrymen who had come in to see the sights. Judging by their faces, they were father and son. The elder, a wrinkled man of perhaps fifty, wore a scant gray beard. The younger had a small box on his shoulder.

At the hour when these strangers entered the public square, a large crowd had gathered, for it was a feast day, and everyone was bent on having a good time. All the people seemed very happy. Some, seated in little open-air booths, were eating, drinking, and smoking. Others were buying odds and ends from the street-vendors, tossing coins, and playing various games of chance.

The two men walked about aimlessly. They seemed to have no friends among the pleasure-seekers. At last, however, as they stood reading a public notice posted at the entrance of the town-hall or *yamen*, a bystander asked them who they were.

"Oh, we are jugglers from a distant province," said the elder, smiling and pointing towards the box. "We can do many tricks for the amusement of the people."

Soon it was spread about among the crowd that two famous jugglers had just arrived from the capital, and that they were able to perform many wonderful deeds. Now it happened that the mandarin or mayor of the city, at that very moment was entertaining a number of guests in the *yamen*. They had just finished eating, and the host was wondering what he should do to amuse his friends, when a servant told him of the jugglers.

"Ask them what they can do," said the mandarin eagerly. "I will pay them well if they can really amuse us, but I want something more than the old tricks of knife-throwing and balancing. They must show us something new."

The servant went outside and spoke to the jugglers: "The great man bids you tell him what you can do. If you can amuse his visitors he will bring them out to the private grandstand, and let you perform before them and the people who are gathered together."

"Tell your honorable master," said the elder, whom we shall call Zhang, "that, try us as he will, he will not be disappointed. Tell him that we come from the unknown land of dreams and visions, that we can turn rocks into mountains, rivers into oceans, mice into elephants, in short, that there is nothing in magic too difficult for us to do."

The official was delighted when he heard the report of his servant. "Now we may have a little fun," he said to his guests, "for there are jugglers outside who will perform their wonderful tricks before us."

The guests filed out on to the grandstand at one side of the public square. The mandarin commanded that a rope should be stretched across so as to leave an open space in full view of the crowd, where the two Zhangs might give their exhibition.

For a time the two strangers entertained the people with some of the simpler tricks, such as spinning plates in the air, tossing bowls up and catching them on chopsticks, making flowers grow from empty pots, and transforming one object into another. At last, however, the mandarin cried out: "These tricks are very good of their kind, but how about those idle boasts of changing rivers into oceans and mice into elephants? Did you not say that you came from the land of dreams? These tricks you have done are stale and shopworn. Have you nothing new with which to regale my guests on this holiday?"

"Most certainly, your excellency. But surely you would not have a laborer do more than his employer requires? Would that not be quite contrary to the teachings of our fathers? Be assured, sir, anything that you demand I can do for you. Only say the word."

The mandarin laughed outright at this boasting language. "Take care, my man! Do not go too far with your promises. There are too many impostors around for me to believe every stranger. Hark you! no lying, for if you lie in the presence of my guests, I shall take great pleasure in having you beaten."

"My words are quite true, your excellency," repeated Zhang earnestly. "What have we to gain by deceit, we who have performed our miracles before the countless hosts of yonder Western Heaven?"

"Ha, ha! hear the braggarts!" shouted the guests. "What shall we command them to do?"

For a moment they consulted together, whispering and laughing.

"I have it," cried the host finally. "Our feast was short of fruit, since this is the off season. Suppose we let this fellow supply us. Here, fellow, produce us a peach, and be quick about it. We have no time for fooling."

"What, masters, a peach?" exclaimed the elder Zhang in mock dismay. "Surely at this season you do not expect a peach."

"Caught at his own game," laughed the guests, and the people began to hoot derisively.

"But, father, you promised to do anything he required," urged the son. "If he asks even a peach, how can you refuse and at the same time save your face?"

"Hear the boy talk," mumbled the father, "and yet, perhaps he's right. Very well, masters," turning to the crowd, "if it's a peach you want, why, a peach you shall have, even though I must send into the garden of the Western Heaven for the fruit."

The people became silent and the mandarin's guests forgot to laugh. The old man, still muttering, opened the box from which he had been taking the magic bowls, plates, and other articles. "To think of people wanting peaches at this season! What is the world coming to?"

After fumbling in the box for some moments he drew out a skein of golden thread, fine spun and as light as gossamer. No sooner had he unwound a portion of this thread than a sudden gust of wind carried it up into the air above the heads of the onlookers. Faster and faster the old man paid out the magic coil, higher and higher the free end rose into the heavens, until, strain his eyes as he would, no one present could see into what far-region it had vanished.

"Wonderful, wonderful!" shouted the people with one voice, "the old man is a fairy."

For a moment they forgot all about the mandarin, the jugglers, and the peach, so amazed were they at beholding the flight of the magic thread.

At last the old man seemed satisfied with the distance to which his cord had sailed, and, with a bow to the spectators, he tied the end to a large wooden pillar which helped to support the roof of the grand stand. For a moment the structure trembled and swayed as if it too would be carried off into the blue ether, the guests turned pale and clutched their chairs for support, but not even the mandarin dared to speak, so sure were they now that they were in the presence of fairies.

"Everything is ready for the journey," said old Zhang calmly.

"What! shall you leave us?" asked the mayor, finding his voice again.

"I? Oh, no, my old bones are not spry enough for quick climbing. My son here will bring us the magic peach. He is handsome and active enough to enter that heavenly garden. Graceful, oh graceful is that peach tree—of course, you remember the line from the poem—and a graceful man must pluck the fruit."

The mandarin was still more surprised at the juggler's knowledge of a famous poem from the classics. It made him and his friends all the more certain that the newcomers were indeed fairies.

The young man at a sign from his father tightened his belt and the bands about his ankles, and then, with a graceful gesture to the astonished people, sprang upon the magic string, balanced himself for a moment on the steep incline, and then ran as nimbly up as a sailor would have mounted a rope ladder. Higher and higher he climbed until he seemed no bigger than a lark ascending into the blue sky, and then, like some tiny speck, far, far away, on the western horizon.

The people gazed in open-mouthed wonder. They were struck dumb and filled with some nameless fear; they hardly dared to look at the enchanter who stood calmly in their midst, smoking his long-stemmed pipe.

The mandarin, ashamed of having laughed at and threatened this man who was clearly a fairy, did not know what to say. He snapped his long finger nails and looked at his guests in mute astonishment. The visitors silently drank their tea, and the crowd of sightseers craned their necks in a vain effort to catch sight of the vanished fairy. Only one in all that assembly, a bright-eyed little boy of eight, dared to break the silence, and he caused a hearty burst of merriment by crying out, "Oh, daddy, will the bad young man fly off into the sky and leave his poor father all alone?"

The graybeard laughed loudly with the others, and tossed the lad a copper. "Ah, the good boy," he said smiling, "he has been well trained to love his father; no fear of foreign ways spoiling his filial piety."

After a few moments of waiting, old Zhang laid aside his pipe and fixed his eyes once more on the western sky. "It is coming," he said quietly. "The peach will soon be here."

Suddenly he held out his hand as if to catch some falling object, but, look as they would, the people could see nothing. Swish! thud! it came like a streak of light, and, lo, there in the magician's fingers was a peach, the most beautiful specimen the people had ever seen, large and rosy. "Straight from the garden of the gods," said Zhang, handing the fruit to the mandarin, "a peach in the Second Moon, and the snow hardly off the ground."

Trembling with excitement, the official took the peach and cut it open. It was large enough for all his guests to have a taste, and such a taste it was! They smacked their lips and wished for more, secretly thinking that never again would ordinary fruit be worth the eating.

But all this time the old juggler, magician, fairy or whatever you choose to call him, was looking anxiously into the sky. The result of this trick was more than he had bargained for. True, he had been able to produce the magic peach which the mandarin had called for, but his son, where was his son? He shaded his eyes and looked far up into the blue heavens, and so did the people, but no one could catch a glimpse of the departed youth.

"Oh, my son, my son," cried the old man in despair, "how cruel is the fate that has robbed me of you, the only prop of my declining years! Oh, my boy, my boy, would that I had not sent you on so perilous a journey! Who now will look after my grave when I am gone?"

Higher and higher he climbed.

Suddenly the silken cord on which the young man had sped so daringly into the sky, gave a quick jerk which almost toppled over the post to which it was tied, and there, before the very eyes of the people, it fell from the lofty height, a silken pile on the ground in front of them.

The graybeard uttered a loud cry and covered his face with his hands. "Alas! the whole story is plain enough," he sobbed. "My boy was caught in the act of plucking the magic peach from the garden of the gods, and they have thrown him into prison. Woe is me! Ah! woe is me!"

The mandarin and his friends were deeply touched by the old man's grief, and tried in vain to comfort him. "Perhaps he will return," they said. "Have courage!"

"Yes, but in what a shape?" replied the magician. "See! even now they are restoring him to his father."

The people looked, and they saw twirling and twisting through the air the young man's arm. It fell upon the ground in front of them at the fairy's feet. Next came the head, a leg, the body. One by one before the gasping, shuddering people, the parts of the unfortunate young man were restored to his father.

After the first outburst of wild, frantic grief the old man by a great effort gained control of his feelings, and began to gather up these parts, putting them tenderly into the wooden box.

By this time many of the spectators were weeping at the sight of the father's affliction. "Come," said the mandarin at last, deeply moved, "let us present the old man with sufficient money to give his boy a decent burial."

All present agreed willingly, for there is no sight in China that causes greater pity than that of an aged parent robbed by death of an only son. The copper cash fell in a shower at the juggler's feet, and soon tears of gratitude were mingled with those of sorrow. He gathered up the money and tied it in a large black cloth. Then a wonderful change came over his face. He seemed all of a sudden to forget his grief. Turning to the box, he raised the lid. The people heard him say: "Come, my son; the crowd is waiting for you to thank them. Hurry up! They have been very kind to us."

In an instant the box was thrown open with a bang, and before the mandarin and his friends, before the eyes of all the sightseers the young man, strong and whole once more, stepped forth and bowed, clasping his hands and giving the national salute.

For a moment all were silent. Then, as the wonder of the whole thing dawned upon them, the people broke forth into a tumult of shouts, laughter, and compliments. "The fairies have surely come to visit us!" they shouted. "The city will be blessed with good fortune! Perhaps it is Fairy Old Boy himself who is among us!

The mandarin rose and addressed the jugglers, thanking them in the name of the city for their visit and for the taste they had given to him and his guests of the peach from the heavenly orchard.

Even as he spoke, the magic box opened again; the two fairies disappeared inside, the lid closed, and the chest rose from the ground above the heads of the people. For a moment it floated around in a circle like some homing pigeon trying to find its bearings before starting on a return journey. Then, with a sudden burst of speed, it shot off into the heavens and vanished from the sight of those below, and not a thing remained as proof of the strange visitors except the magic peach seed that lay beside the teacups on the mandarin's table.

According to the most ancient writings there is now nothing left to tell of this story. It has been declared, however, by later scholars that the official and his friends who had eaten the magic peach, at once began to feel a change in their lives. While, before the coming of the fairies, they had lived unfairly, accepting bribes and taking part in many shameful practices, now, after tasting of the heavenly fruit, they began to grow better. The people soon began to honor and love them, saying, "Surely these great men are not like others of their kind, for these men are just and honest in their dealings with us. They seem not to be ruling for their own reward!"

However this may be, we do know that before many years their city became the center of the greatest peach-growing section of China, and even yet when strangers walk in the orchards and look up admiringly at the beautiful sweet-smelling fruit, the natives sometimes ask proudly, "And have you never heard about the wonderful peach which was the beginning of all our orchards, the magic peach the fairies brought us from the Western Heaven?"

NCE a ship loaded with pleasure-seekers was sailing from North China to Shanghai. High winds and stormy weather had delayed her, and she was still one week from port when a great plague broke out on board. This plague was of the worst kind. It attacked passengers and sailors alike until there were so few left to sail the vessel that it seemed as if she would soon be left to the mercy of winds and waves.

On all sides lay the dead, and the groans of the dying were most terrible to hear. Of that great company of travelers only one, a little boy named Yingluo, had escaped. At last the few sailors, who had been trying hard to save their ship, were obliged to lie down upon the deck, a prey to the dreadful sickness, and soon they too were dead.

Yingluo now found himself alone on the sea. For some reason—he did not know why—the gods or the sea fairies had spared him, but as he looked about in terror at the friends and loved ones who had died, he almost wished that he might join them.

The sails flapped about like great broken wings, while the giant waves dashed higher above the deck, washing many of the bodies overboard and wetting the little boy to the skin. Shivering with cold, he gave himself up for lost and prayed to the gods, whom his mother had often told him about, to take him from this dreadful ship and let him escape the fatal illness.

As he lay there praying he heard a slight noise in the rigging just above his head. Looking up, he saw a ball of fire running along a yardarm near the top of the mast. The sight was so strange that he forgot his prayer and stared with open-mouthed wonder. To his astonishment, the ball grew brighter and brighter, and then suddenly began slipping down the mast, all the time increasing in size. The poor boy did not know what to do or to think. Were the gods, in answer to his prayer, sending fire to burn the vessel? If so, he would soon escape. Anything would be better than to be alone upon the sea.

Nearer and nearer came the fireball. At last, when it reached the deck, to Yingluo's surprise, something very, very strange happened. Before he had time to feel alarmed, the light vanished, and a funny little man stood in front of him peering anxiously into the child's frightened face.

"Yes, you are the lad I'm looking for," he said at last, speaking in a piping voice that almost made Yingluo smile. "You are Yingluo, and you are the only one left of this wretched company." This he said, pointing towards the bodies lying here and there about the deck.

Although he saw that the old man meant him no harm, the child could say nothing, but waited in silence, wondering what would happen next.

By this time the vessel was tossing and pitching so violently that it seemed every minute as if it would upset and go down beneath the foaming waves, never to rise again. Not many miles distant on the right, some jagged rocks stuck out of the water, lifting their cruel heads as if waiting for the helpless ship.

The newcomer walked slowly towards the mast and tapped on it three times with an iron staff he had been using as a cane. Immediately the sails spread, the vessel righted itself and began to glide over the sea so fast that the gulls were soon left far behind, while the threatening rocks upon which the ship had been so nearly dashed seemed like specks in the distance.

"Do you remember me?" said the stranger, suddenly turning and coming up to Yingluo, but his voice was lost in the whistling of the wind, and the boy knew only by the moving of his lips that the old man was talking. The graybeard bent over until his mouth was at Yingluo's ear: "Did you ever see me before?"

With a puzzled look, at first the child shook his head. Then as he gazed more closely there seemed to be something that he recognized about the wrinkled face. "Yes, I think so, but I don't know when."

With a tap of his staff the fairy stopped the blowing of the wind, and then spoke once more to his small companion: "One year ago I passed through your village. I was dressed in rags, and was begging my way along the street, trying to find someone who would feel sorry for me. Alas! no one answered my cry for mercy. Not a crust was thrown into my bowl. All the people were deaf, and fierce dogs drove me from door to door. Finally when I was almost dying of hunger, I began to feel that here was a village without one good person in it. Just then you saw my suffering, ran into the house, and brought me out food. Your heartless mother saw you doing this and beat you cruelly. Do you remember now, my child?"

"Yes, I remember," he answered sadly, "and that mother is now lying dead. Alas! all, all are dead, my father and my brothers also. Not one is left of my family."

"Little did you know, my boy, to whom you were giving food that day. You took me for a lowly beggar, but, behold, it was not a poor man that you fed, for I am Iron Staff. You must have heard of me when they were telling of the fairies in the Western Heaven, and of their adventures here on earth."

"Yes, yes," answered Yingluo, trembling half with fear and half with joy, "indeed I have heard of you many, many times, and all the people love you for your kind deeds of mercy."

"Alas! they did not show their love, my little one. Surely you know that if anyone wishes to reward the fairies for their mercies, he must begin to do deeds of the same kind himself. No one but you in all your village had pity on me in my rags. If they had known that I was Iron Staff, everything would have been different; they would have given me a feast and begged for my protection.

"The only love that loves aright
Is that which loves in every plight.
The beggar in his sad array
Is molded of the selfsame clay.
"Who knows a man by what he wears,
By what he says or by his prayers?
Hidden beneath that wrinkled skin
A fairy may reside within.
"Then treat with kindness and with love
The lowly man, the god above;

A friendly nod, a welcome smile—
For love is ever worth the while."

Yingluo listened in wonder to Iron Staff's little poem, and when he had finished, the boy's face was glowing with the love of which the fairy had spoken. "My poor, poor father and mother!" he cried; "they knew nothing of these beautiful things you are telling me. They were brought up in poverty. As they were knocked about in childhood by those around them, so they learned to beat others who begged them for help. Is it strange that they did not have hearts full of pity for you when you looked like a beggar?"

"But what about you, my boy? You were not deaf when I asked you. Have you not been whipped and punished all your life? How then did you learn to look with love at those in tears?"

The child could not answer these questions, but only looked sorrowfully at Iron Staff. "Oh, can you not, good fairy, will you not restore my parents and brothers, and give them another chance to be good and useful people?"

"Listen, Yingluo; it is impossible—unless you do two things first," he answered, stroking his beard gravely and leaning heavily upon his staff.

"What are they? What must I do to save my family? Anything you ask of me will not be too much to pay for your kindness."

"First you must tell me of some good deed done by these people for whose lives you are asking. Name only one, for that will be enough; but it is against our rules to help those who have done nothing."

Yingluo was silent, and for a moment his face was clouded. "Yes, I know," he said finally, brightening. "They burned incense once at the temple. That was certainly a deed of virtue."

"But when was it, little one, that they did this?"

"When my big brother was sick, and they were praying for him to get well. The doctors could not save him with boiled turnip juice or with any other of the medicines they used, so my parents begged the gods."

"Selfish, selfish!" muttered Iron Staff. "If their eldest son had not been dying they would have spent no money at the temple. They tried in this way to buy back his health, for they were expecting him to support them in their old age."

Yingluo's face fell. "You are right," he answered.

"Can you think of nothing else?

"Yes, oh, yes, last year when the foreigner rode through our village and fell sick in front of our house, they took him in and cared for him."

"How long?" asked the other sharply.

"Until he died the next week."

"And what did they do with the mule he was riding, his bed, and the money in his bag? Did they try to restore them to his people?"

"No, they said they'd keep them to pay for the trouble." Yingluo's face turned scarlet.

"But try again, dear boy! Is there not one little deed of goodness that was not selfish? Think once more."

For a long time Yingluo did not reply. At length he spoke in a low voice; "I think of one, but I fear it amounts to nothing."

"No good, my child, is too small to be counted when the gods are weighing a man's heart."

"She also went to the temple, with a faithful old servant, and prayed to heaven."

"Last spring the birds were eating in my father's garden. My mother wanted to buy poison from the shop to destroy them, but my father said no, that the little things must live, and he for one was not in favor of killing them."

"At last, Yingluo, you have named a real deed of mercy, and as he spared the tiny birds from poison, so shall his life and the lives of your mother and brothers be restored from the deadly plague.

"But remember there is one other thing that depends on you."

Yingluo's eyes glistened gratefully. "Then if it rests with me, and I can do it, you have my promise. No sacrifice should be too great for a son to make for his loved ones even though his life itself is asked in payment."

"Very well, Yingluo. What I require is that you carry out to the letter my instructions. Now it is time for me to keep my promise to you."

So saying, Iron Staff called on Yingluo to point out the members of his family, and, approaching them one by one, with the end of his iron stick he touched their foreheads. In an instant each, without a word, arose. Looking around and recognizing Yingluo, they stood back, frightened at seeing him with the fairy. When the last had risen to his feet, Iron Staff beckoned all of them to listen. This they did willingly, too much terrified to speak, for they saw on all sides signs of the plague that had swept over the vessel, and they remembered the frightful agony they had suffered in dying. Each knew that he had been lifted by some magic power from darkness into light.

"My friends," began the fairy, "little did you think when less than a year ago you drove me from your door that soon you yourselves would be in need of mercy. Today you have had a peep into the awful land of Yama. You have seen the horror of his tortures, have heard the screams of his slaves, and by another night you would have been carried before him to be judged. What power is it that has saved you from his clutches? As you look back through your wicked lives can you think of any reason why you deserved this rescue? No, there is no memory of goodness in your black hearts. Well, I shall tell you: it is this little boy, this Yingluo, who many times has felt the weight of your wicked hands and has hidden in terror at your coming. To him alone you owe my help."

Father, mother, and brothers all gazed in turn, first at the fairy and then at the timid child whose eyes fell before their looks of gratitude.

"By reason of his goodness this child whom you have scorned is worthy of a place within the Western Heaven. In truth, I came this very day to lead him to that fairyland. For you, however, he wishes to make a sacrifice. With sorrow I am yielding to his wishes. His sacrifice will be that of giving up a place among the fairies and of continuing to live here on this earth with you. He will try to make a change within your household. If at any time you treat him badly and do not heed his wishes—mark you well my words—by the power of this magic staff which I shall place in his hands, he may enter at once into the land of the fairies, leaving you to die in your wickedness. This I command him to do, and he has promised to obey my slightest wish.

"This plague took you off suddenly and ended your wicked lives. Yingluo has raised you from its grasp and his power can lift you from the bed of sin. No other hand than his can bear the rod which I am leaving. If one of you but touch it, instantly he will fall dead upon the ground.

"And now, my child, the time has come for me to leave you. First, however, I must show you what you are now able to do. Around you lie the corpses of sailors and passengers. Tap three times upon the mast and wish that they shall come to life." So saying he handed Yingluo the iron staff.

Although the magic rod was heavy, the child lifted it as if it were a fairy's wand. Then, stepping forward to the mast, he rapped three times as he had been commanded. Immediately on all sides arose the bodies, once more full of life and strength.

"Now command the ship to take you back to your home port, for such sinful creatures as these are in no way fit to make a journey among strangers. They must first return and free their homes of sin."

Again rapping on the mast, the child willed the great vessel to take its homeward course. No sooner had he moved the staff than, like a bird wheeling in the heavens, the bark swung around and started on the return journey. Swifter than a flash of lightning flew the boat, for it was now become a fairy vessel. Before the sailors and the travelers could recover from their surprise, land was sighted and they saw that they were indeed entering the harbor.

Just as the ship was darting toward the shore the fairy suddenly, with a parting word to Yingluo, changed into a flaming ball of fire which rolled along the deck and ascended the spars. Then, as it reached the top of the rigging, it floated off into the blue sky, and all on board, speechless with surprise, watched it until it vanished.

With a cry of thanksgiving, Yingluo flung his arms about his parents and descended with them to the shore.

THE WOODEN TABLET

ES, my boy, whatever happens, be sure to save that tablet. It is the only thing we have left worth keeping."

Kangpu's father was just setting out for the city, to be gone all day. He had been telling Kangpu about some work in the little garden, for the boy was a strong and willing helper.

"All right, father, I'll do what you tell me; but suppose the foreign soldiers should come while you are gone? I heard that they were over at Tang Shu yesterday and burned the village. If they should come here, what must I do?"

Mr. Lin laughed heartily. "Why, there's nothing here for them to burn, if it comes to that!—a mud house, a grass roof, and a pile of ragged bedding. Surely they won't bother my little hut. It's loot they're after—money—or something they can sell."

"But, father," persisted the boy, "haven't you forgotten? Surely you wouldn't wish them to burn your father's tablet?"

"Quite right; for the moment I did forget. Yes, yes, my boy, whatever happens be sure to save the tablet. It is the only thing we have worth keeping."

With that, Mr. Lin went out at the gate, leaving Kangpu standing all alone. The little fellow was scarcely twelve years old. He had a bright, sunny face and a happy heart. Being left by himself did not mean tears and idleness for him.

He went into the poor little house and stood for a moment looking earnestly at the wooden tablet. It was on a shelf in the one-roomed shanty, an oblong piece of wood about twelve inches high, enclosed in a wooden case. Through the carved screen work in the front, Kangpu could see his grandfather's name written in Chinese characters on the tablet. Ever since babyhood Kangpu had been taught to look at this piece of wood with a feeling of reverence.

"Your grandfather's spirit is inside," his father had said one day. "You must worship his spirit, for he was a good man, far better than your dad. If I had obeyed him in all things, I, his only son, should not now be living in this miserable hut."

"But didn't he live here, too?" asked Kangpu in surprise.

"Oh, no, we lived in a big house over yonder in another village; in a big house with a high stone wall."

The little fellow had gasped with surprise at hearing this, for there was not such a thing as a stone wall in his village, and he felt that his grandfather must have been a rich man. He had not asked any more questions, but from that day on he had been rather afraid of the carved wooden box in which his grandfather's spirit was supposed to live.

So, on this day when his father left him alone, the boy stood looking at the tablet, wondering how a big man's spirit could squeeze into such a small space. He put out his finger cautiously and touched the bottom of the box, then drew back, half-frightened at his own daring. No bad results followed. It seemed just like any other piece of wood. Somewhat puzzled, he walked out of the house into the little garden. His father had told him to re-set some young cabbages. This was work which Kangpu had done many times before. First, he gathered a basket of chicken feathers, for his father had told him that a few feathers placed at the roots of the young plant would do more to make it strong and healthy than anything else that could be used.

All day Kangpu worked steadily in the garden. He was just beginning to feel tired, when he heard a woman screaming in the distance. He dropped his basket and rushed to the gate. Down the road at the far side of the village he saw a crowd of women and children running hither and thither, and—yes! there were the soldiers—the dreaded foreign soldiers! They were burning the houses; they were stealing whatever they could find.

Now, most boys would have been frightened—would have taken to their heels without thought of consequences. Kangpu, however, though like other lads afraid of soldiers, was too brave to run without first doing his duty. He decided to stand his ground until he was sure the foreigners were coming his way. Perhaps they would grow tired of their cruel sport and leave the little house unharmed. He watched with wide-open eyes the work of pillage. Alas! these men did not seem to tire of their amusement. One after another the houses were entered and robbed. Women were screaming and children crying. Nearly all the village men were away in a distant market town, for none of them had expected an attack.

Nearer and nearer came the robbers. At last they were next door to Kangpu's hut, and he knew the time had come for him to do his duty. Seizing the basket of chicken feathers, he rushed into the house, snatched the precious tablet from the shelf, and hid it in the bottom of the basket. Then, without stopping to say goodbye to the spot which he had known all his life, he rushed out of the gate and down the narrow street.

"Kill the kid!" shouted a soldier, whom Kangpu nearly ran against in his hurry. "Put down the basket, boy! No stealing here."

"Yes, kill him!" shouted another with a loud laugh; "he'd make a good bit of bacon."

But no one touched him, and Kangpu, still holding tightly to his burden, was soon far out on the winding road among the cornfields. If they should follow, he thought of hiding among the giant cornstalks. His legs were tired now, and he sat down under a stone memorial arch near some crossroads to rest.

Where was he going, and what should he do? These were the questions that filled the boy's whirling little brain. First, he must find out if the soldiers were really destroying all the houses in his village. Perhaps some of them would not be burned and he could return at night to join his father.

After several failures he managed to climb one of the stone pillars and from the arch above he could get a good view of the surrounding country. Over to the west was his village. His heart beat fast when he saw that a great cloud of smoke was rising from the houses. Clearly, the thieves were making quick work of the place, and soon there would be nothing left but piles of mud, brick, ashes and other rubbish.

Night came on. Kangpu clambered down from his stone perch. He was beginning to feel hungry, and yet he dared not turn back towards home. And besides, would not all the other villagers be hungry, too? He lay down at the foot of the stone monument, placing the basket within reach at one side. Soon he fell fast asleep.

How long he had been sleeping he never knew; but it was not yet day when he awoke with a start and looked around him in the moonlight. Someone had called him distinctly by name. At first, he thought it must have been his father's voice; and then as he grew wider and wider awake he knew this could not be, for the voice sounded like that of an old man. Kangpu looked around in amazement, first at the stone columns, then at the arch above. No one was to be seen. Had he been dreaming?

Just as he lay back to sleep once more, the voice sounded again very faintly, "Kangpu! Kangpu! why don't you let me out? I can't breathe under all these feathers."

Quick as a flash he knew what was the matter. Burying his hand in the basket, he seized the wooden tablet, drew it from its hiding-place, and stood it up on the stone base. Wonder of wonders! There before his very eyes he saw a tiny fellow, not six inches high, sitting on top of the wooden upright and dangling his legs over the front of the tablet. The dwarf had a long gray beard, and Kangpu, without looking twice, knew that this was the spirit of his dead grandfather come to life and clothed with flesh and blood.

"Ho, ho!" said the small man, laughing, "so you thought you'd bury your old grandfather in feathers, did you? A soft enough grave, but rather smelly."

"But, sir," cried Kangpu, "I had to do it, to save you from the soldiers! They were just about to burn our house and you in it."

"There, there, my boy! don't be uneasy. I am not scolding you. You did the best you could for your old gran'ther. If you had been like most lads, you would have taken to your heels and left me to those sea-devils who were sacking the village. There is no doubt about it: you saved me from a second death much more terrible than the first one."

Kangpu shuddered, for he knew that his grandfather had been killed in battle. He had heard his father tell the story many times.

"Now, what do you propose doing about it?" asked the old man finally, looking straight into the boy's face.

"Doing about it, sir? Why, really, I don't know. I thought that perhaps in the morning the soldiers would be gone and I could carry you back. Surely my father will be looking for me."

"What! looking for you in the ashes? And what could he do if he did find you? Your house is burned, your chickens carried away and your cabbages trampled underfoot. A sorry home he will return to. You would be just one more mouth to feed. No! that plan will never do. If your father thinks you are dead, he will go off to another province to get work. That would save him from starvation."

"But what am I to do?" wailed poor Kangpu. "I don't want him to leave me all alone!"

"All alone! What! don't you count your old grand-daddy? Surely you are not a very polite youngster, even if you did save me from burning to death."

"Count you?" repeated the boy, surprised. "Why, surely you can't help me to earn a living?"

"Why not, boy? Is this an age when old men are good for nothing?"

"But, sir, you are only the *spirit* of my grandfather, and spirits cannot work!"

"Ha, ha! just hear the child. Why, look you, I will show you what spirits can do, provided you will do exactly what I tell you."

Of course, Kangpu promised, for he was always obedient; and was not this little man who spoke so strangely, the spirit of his grandfather? And is not every lad in China taught to honor his ancestors?

"Now, listen, my boy. First, let me say that if you had not been kind, brave and filial, I should not take the trouble to help you out of your misfortune. As it is, there is nothing else for me to do. I cast your father off because he was disobedient. He has lived in a dirty hovel ever since. Doubtless, he has been sorry for his misdeeds, for I see that although he was disgraced by being sent away from the family home, he has taught you to honor and love me. Most boys would have snatched up a blanket or a piece of bread before running from the enemy, but you thought only of my tablet. You saved me and went to bed hungry. For this bravery, I shall give back to you the home of your ancestors."

"But I can't live in it," said Kangpu, full of wonder, "if you will not let my father come back to it. If he goes away he will have a very hard time: he will be lonely without me, and may die; and then I would not be able to take care of his grave, or to burn incense there at the proper season!"

"Quite right, Kangpu. I see you love your father as well as your grandfather's tablet. Very well; you shall have your way. I daresay your father is sorry by this time that he treated me so badly."

"Indeed, he must be," said the boy earnestly, "for I have seen him kneel before your tablet many times and burn incense there on the proper days. I know he is very sorry."

"Very well; go to sleep again. Let us wait until morning and then I shall see what I can do for you. This moonlight is not bright enough for my old eyes. I shall have to wait for morning."

As he spoke these last words, the little man began to grow smaller and smaller before the eyes of his grandson, until at last he had altogether disappeared.

At first, Kangpu was too much excited to close his eyes. He remained for a time looking up into the starry sky and wondering if what he had heard would really come true, or whether he could have dreamt the whole story of his grandfather's coming to life again. Could it really be that the old family property would be given back to his father? He remembered now that he had once heard his father speak of having lived in a large house on a beautiful compound. It was just before Kangpu's mother had been carried away by the fever. As she had lain tossing upon the rude stone bed, with none of those comforts which are so necessary for the sick, Kangpu remembered that his father had said to her: "What a shame that we are not living in my father's house! There you might have had every luxury. It is all my fault; I disobeyed my father."

Soon after that his mother had died, but Kangpu had remembered those words ever since, and had often wished that he could hear more about this house where his father had spent his boyhood. Could it be possible that they would soon be living in it? No, surely there must be some mistake: the night fairies of his dreams had been deceiving him. With a sigh he closed his eyes and once more fell asleep.

When Kangpu next awoke, the sun was shining full in his face. He looked around him, sleepily rubbing his eyes and trying to remember all that had happened. Suddenly he thought of the tablet and of his grandfather's appearance at midnight. But, strange to say, the basket had disappeared with all its contents. The tablet was nowhere to be seen, and even the stone arch under which he had gone to sleep had completely vanished. Alas! his grandfather's tablet—how poorly he had guarded it! What terrible thing would happen now that it was gone!

Kangpu stood up and looked around him in trembling surprise. What could have taken place while he was sleeping? At first, he did not know what to do. Fortunately, the path through the corn was still there, and he decided to return to the village and see if he could find any trace of his father. His talk with the old man must have been only an idle dream, and some thief must have carried off the basket. If only the stone arch had not vanished Kangpu would not have been so perplexed.

He hurried along the narrow road, trying to forget the empty stomach which was beginning to cry for food. If the soldiers were still in the village, surely they would not hurt an empty-handed little boy. More than likely they had gone the day before. If he could only find his father! Now he crossed the little brook where the women came to rub their clothes upon the rocks. There was the big mulberry tree where the boys used to gather leaves for their silkworms. Another turn of the road and he would see the village.

When Kangpu passed around the corner and looked for the ruins of the village hovels, an amazing sight met his gaze. There, rising directly before him, was a great stone wall, like those he had seen around the rich people's houses when his father had taken him to the city. The great gate stood wide open, and the keeper, rushing out, exclaimed:

"Ah! the little master has come!"

Completely bewildered, the boy followed the servant through the gateway, passed through several wide courts, and then into a garden where flowers and strangely-twisted trees were growing.

This, then, was the house which his grandfather had promised him—the home of his ancestors. Ah! how beautiful! how beautiful! Many men and women servants bowed low as he passed, saluting with great respect and crying out:

"Yes, it is really the little master! He has come back to his own!"

Kangpu, seeing how well dressed the servants were, felt much ashamed of his own ragged garments, and put up his hands to hide a torn place. What was his amazement to find that he was no longer clad in soiled, ragged clothes, that he was dressed in the handsomest embroidered silk. From head to foot he was fitted out like the young Prince his father had pointed out to him one day in the city.

Then they entered a magnificent reception-hall on the other side of the garden. Kangpu could not keep back his tears, for there stood his father waiting to meet him.

"My boy! my boy!" cried the father, "you have come back to me. I feared you had been stolen away forever."

"Oh, no!" said Kangpu, "you have not lost me, but I have lost the tablet. A thief came and took it last night while I was sleeping."

"Lost the tablet! A thief! Why, no, my son, you are mistaken! There it is, just before you."

Kangpu looked, and saw standing on a handsome carved table the very thing he had mourned as lost. As he stared in surprise he almost expected to see the tiny figure swinging its legs over the top, and to hear the high-pitched voice of his grandfather.

"Yes, it is really the lost tablet!" he cried joyfully. "How glad I am it is back in its rightful place once more."

Then father and son fell upon their knees before the wooden emblem, and bowed reverently nine times to the floor, thanking the spirit for all it had done for them. When they arose their hearts were full of a new happiness.

THE GOLDEN NUGGET

NCE upon a time many, many years ago, there lived in China two friends named Qiwu and Baoshu. These two young men, like Damon and Pythias, loved each other and were always together. No cross words passed between them; no unkind thoughts marred their friendship. Many an interesting tale might be told of their unselfishness, and of how the good fairies gave them the true reward of virtue. One story alone, however, will be enough to show how strong was their affection and their goodness.

It was a bright beautiful day in early spring when Qiwu and Baoshu set out for a stroll together, for they were tired of the city and its noises.

"Let us go into the heart of the pine forest," said Qiwu lightly. "There we can forget the cares that worry us; there we can breathe the sweetness of the flowers and lie on the moss-covered ground."

"Good!" said Baoshu, "I, too, am tired. The forest is the place for rest."

Happy as two lovers on a holiday, they passed along the winding road, their eyes turned in longing toward the distant tree-tops. Their hearts beat fast in youthful pleasure as they drew nearer and nearer to the woods.

"For thirty days I have worked over my books," sighed Qiwu. "For thirty days I have not had a rest. My head is stuffed so full of wisdom, that I am afraid it will burst. Oh, for a breath of the pure air blowing through the greenwood."

"And I," added Baoshu sadly, "have worked like a slave at my counter and found it just as dull as you have found your books. My master treats me badly. It seems good, indeed, to get beyond his reach."

Now they came to the border of the grove, crossed a little stream, and plunged headlong among the trees and shrubs. For many an hour they rambled on, talking and laughing merrily; when suddenly on passing around a clump of flower-covered bushes, they saw shining in the pathway directly in front of them a lump of gold.

"See!" said both, speaking at the same time, and pointing toward the treasure.

Qiwu, stooping, picked up the nugget. It was nearly as large as a lemon, and was very pretty. "It is yours, my dear friend," said he, at the same time handing it to Baoshu; "yours because you saw it first."

"No, no," answered Baoshu, "you are wrong, my brother, for you were first to speak. Now, you can never say hereafter that the good fairies have not rewarded you for all your faithful hours of study."

"Repaid me for my study! Why, that is impossible. Are not the wise men always saying that study brings its own reward? No, the gold is yours: I insist upon it. Think of your weeks of hard labor—of the masters that have ground you to the bone! Here is something far better. Take it," laughing. "May it be the nest egg by means of which you may hatch out a great fortune."

Thus they joked for some minutes, each refusing to take the treasure for himself; each insisting that it belonged to the other. At last, the chunk of gold was dropped in the very spot where they had first spied it, and the two comrades went away, each happy because he loved his friend better than anything else in the world. Thus they turned their backs on any chance of quarrelling.

They saw shining in the pathway, directly in front of them, a lump of gold.

"It was not for gold that we left the city," exclaimed Qiwu warmly.

"No," replied his friend, "One day in this forest is worth a thousand nuggets."

"Let us go to the spring and sit down on the rocks," suggested Qiwu. "It is the coolest spot in the whole grove."

When they reached the spring they were sorry to find the place already occupied. A countryman was stretched at full length on the ground.

"Wake up, fellow!" cried Baoshu, "there is money for you nearby. Up yonder path a golden apple is waiting for some man to go and pick it up."

Then they described to the unwelcome stranger the exact spot where the treasure was, and were delighted to see him set out in eager search.

For an hour they enjoyed each other's company, talking of all the hopes and ambitions of their future, and listening to the music of the birds that hopped about on the branches overhead.

At last they were startled by the angry voice of the man who had gone after the nugget. "What trick is this you have played on me, masters? Why do you make a poor man like me run his legs off for nothing on a hot day?"

"What do you mean, fellow?" asked Qiwu, astonished. "Did you not find the fruit we told you about?"

"No," he answered, in a tone of half-hidden rage, "but in its place a monster snake, which I cut in two with my blade. Now, the gods will bring me bad luck for killing something in the woods. If you thought you could drive me from this place by such a trick, you'll soon find you were mistaken, for I was first upon this spot and you have no right to give me orders."

"Stop your chatter, bumpkin, and take this copper for your trouble. We thought we were doing you a favor. If you are blind, there's no one but yourself to blame. Come, Baoshu, let us go back and have a look at this wonderful snake that has been hiding in a chunk of gold."

Laughing merrily, the two companions left the countryman and turned back in search of the nugget.

"If I am not mistaken," said the student, "the gold lies beyond that fallen tree."

"Quite true; we shall soon see the dead snake."

Quickly they crossed the remaining stretch of pathway, with their eyes fixed intently on the ground. Arriving at the spot where they had left the shining treasure, what was their surprise to see, not the lump of gold, not the dead snake described by the idler, but, instead, two beautiful golden nuggets, each larger than the one they had seen at first.

Each friend picked up one of these treasures and handed it joyfully to his companion.

"At last the fairies have rewarded you for your unselfishness!" said Qiwu.

"Yes," answered Baoshu, "by granting me a chance to give you your deserts."

THE MAN WHO WOULD NOT SCOLD

LD Wang lived in a village near Nanjing. He cared for nothing in the world but to eat good food and plenty of it. Now, though this Wang was by no means a poor man, it made him very sad to spend money, and so people called him in sport, the Miser King, for Wang is the Chinese word for king. His greatest pleasure was to eat at someone else's table when he knew that the food would cost him nothing, and you may be sure that at such times he always licked his chopsticks clean. But when he was spending his own money, he tightened his belt and drank a great deal of water, eating very little but scraps such as his friends would have thrown to the dogs. Thus people laughed at him and said:

> "When Wang an invitation gets,
> He chews and chews until he sweats,
> But, when his own food he must eat.
> The tears flow down and wet his feet."

One day while Wang was lying half asleep on the bank of a stream that flowed near his house he began to feel hungry. He had been in that spot all day without tasting anything. At last he saw a flock of ducks swimming in the river. He knew that they belonged to a rich man named Lin who lived in the village. They were fat ducks, so plump and tempting that it made him hungry to look at them. "Oh, for a boiled duck!" he said to himself with a sigh. "Why is it that the gods have not given me a taste of duck during the past year? What have I done to be thus denied?"

Then the thought flashed into his mind: "Here am I asking why the gods have not given me ducks to eat. Who knows but that they have sent this flock thinking I would have sense enough to grab one? Friend Lin, many thanks for your kindness. I think I shall accept your offer and take one of these fowls for my dinner." Of course Mr. Lin was nowhere near to hear old Wang thanking him.

By this time the flock had come to shore. The miser picked himself up lazily from the ground, and, after tiring himself out, he at last managed to pick one of the ducks up, too. He took it home joyfully, hiding it under his ragged garment. Once in his own yard, he lost no time in killing and preparing it for dinner. He ate it, laughing to himself all the time at his own slyness, and wondering what his friend Lin would think if he chanced to count his ducks that night. "No doubt he will believe it was a giant hawk that carried off that bird," he said, chuckling. "My word! but didn't I do a great trick? I think I will repeat the dose tomorrow. The first duck is well lodged in my stomach, and I am ready to take an oath that all the others will find a bed in the same boarding-house before many weeks are past. It would be a pity to leave the first one to pine away in lonely grief. I could never be so cruel."

So old Wang went to bed happy. For several hours he snored away noisily, dreaming that a certain rich man had promised him good food all the rest of his life, and that he would never be forced to do another stroke of work. At midnight, however, he was awakened from his sleep by an unpleasant itching. His whole body seemed to be on fire, and the pain was more than he could bear. He got up and paced the floor. There was no oil in the house for his lamp, and he had to wait until morning to see what was the matter. At early dawn he stepped outside his shanty. Lo, and behold! he found little red spots all over his body. Before his very eyes he saw tiny duck feathers sprouting from these spots. As the morning went by, the feathers grew larger and larger, until his whole body was covered with them from head to foot. Only his face and hands were free of the strange growth.

With a cry of horror, Wang began to pull the feathers out by handfuls, flinging them in the dirt and stamping on them. "The gods have fooled me!" he yelled. "They made me take the duck and eat it, and now they are punishing me for stealing." But the faster he jerked the feathers out, the faster they grew in again, longer and more glossy than before. Then, too, the pain was so great that he could scarcely keep from rolling on the ground. At last completely worn out by his useless labor, and moaning with despair, he took to his bed. "Am I to be changed into a bird?" he groaned. "May the gods have mercy on me!"

He tossed about on his bed: he could not sleep; his heart was sick with fear. Finally he fell into a troubled sleep, and, sleeping, had a dream. A fairy came to his bedside; it was Fairy Old Boy, the friend of the people. "Ah, my poor Wang," said the fairy, "all this trouble you have brought upon yourself by your shiftless, lazy habits. When others work, why do you lie down and sleep your time away? Why don't you get up and shake your lazy legs? There is no place in the world for such a man as you except the pig-sty."

"I know you are telling the truth," wailed Wang, "but how, oh, how can I ever work with all these feathers sticking out of me? They will kill me! They will kill me!"

"Hear the man!" laughed Old Boy. "Now, if you were a hopeful, happy fellow, you would say, 'What a stroke of luck! No need to buy garments. The gods have given me a suit of clothes that will never wear out.' You are a pretty fellow to be complaining, aren't you?"

After joking in this way for a little while, the good fairy changed his tone of voice and said, "Now, Wang, are you really sorry for the way you have lived, sorry for your years of idleness, sorry because you disgraced your old Father and Mother? I hear your parents died of hunger because you would not help them."

Wang, seeing that Old Boy knew all about his past life, and, feeling his pain growing worse and worse every minute, cried out at last: "Yes! Yes! I will do anything you say. Only, I pray you, free me of these feathers!"

"I wouldn't have your feathers," said Old Boy, "and I cannot free you of them. You will have to do the whole thing yourself. What you need is to hear a good scolding. Go and get Mr. Lin, the owner of the stolen duck, to scold freely. The harder he scolds, the sooner will your feathers drop out."

Now, of course, some readers will laugh and say, "But this was only a silly dream, and meant nothing." Mr. Wang, however, did not think in this way. He woke up very happy. He would go to Mr. Lin, confess everything and take the scolding. Then he would be free of his feathers and would go to work. Truly he had led a lazy life. What the good Fairy Old Boy had said about his father and mother had hurt him very badly, for he knew that every word was true. From this day on, he would not be lazy; he would take a wife and become the father of a family.

Miser Wang meant all right when he started out from his shanty. From his little hoard of money he took enough cash to pay Mr. Lin for the stolen duck. He would do everything the fairy had told him and even more. But this doing more was just where he got into trouble. As he walked along the road jingling the string of cash, and thinking that he must soon give it up to his neighbor, he grew very sad. He loved every copper of his money and he disliked to part with it. After all, Old Boy had not told him he must confess to the owner of the duck; he had said he must go to Lin and get Lin to give a good scolding. "Old Boy did not say that Lin must scold *me*," thought the miser. "All that I need do is to get him to *scold*, and then my feathers will drop off and I shall be happy. Why not tell him that old Sen stole his duck, and get him to give Sen a scolding? That will surely do just as well, and I shall save my money as well as my face. Besides, if I tell Lin that I am a thief, perhaps he will send for a policeman and they will haul me off to prison. Surely going to jail would be as bad as wearing feathers. Ha, ha! This will be a good joke on Sen, Lin, and the whole lot of them. I shall fool Fairy Old Boy too. Really he had no right to speak of my father and mother in the way he did. After all, they died of fever, and I was no doctor to cure them. How could he say it was my fault?"

The longer Wang talked to himself, the surer he became that it was useless to tell Lin that he had stolen the duck. By the time he had reached the duck man's house he had fully made up his mind to deceive him. Mr. Lin invited him to come in and sit down. He was a plain-spoken, honest kind of man, this Lin. Everybody liked him, for he never spoke ill of any man and he always had something good to say of his neighbors.

"Well, what's your business, friend Wang? You have come out bright and early, and it's a long walk from your place to mine."

"Oh, I had something important I wanted to talk to you about," began Wang slyly. "That's a fine flock of ducks you have over in the meadow."

"Yes," said Mr. Lin smiling, "a fine flock indeed." But he said nothing of the stolen fowl.

"How many have you?" questioned Wang more boldly.

"I counted them yesterday morning and there were fifteen."

"But did you count them again last night?"

"Yes, I did," answered Lin slowly.

"And there were only fourteen then?"

"Quite right, friend Wang, one of them was missing; but one duck is of little importance. Why do you speak of it?"

"What, no importance! losing a duck? How can you say so? A duck's a duck, isn't it, and surely you would like to know how you lost it?"

"A hawk most likely."

"No, it wasn't a hawk, but if you would go and look in old Sen's duck yard, you would likely find feathers."

"Nothing more natural, I am sure, in a duck yard."

"Yes, but your duck's feathers," persisted Wang.

"What! you think old Sen is a thief, do you, and that he has been stealing from me?"

"Exactly! you have it now."

"Well, well, that is too bad! I am sorry the old fellow is having such a hard time. He is a good worker and deserves better luck. I should willingly have given him the duck if he had only asked for it. Too bad that he had to steal it."

Wang waited to see how Mr. Lin planned to punish the thief, feeling sure that the least he could do, would be to go and give him a good scolding.

But nothing of the kind happened. Instead of growing angry, Mr. Lin seemed to be sorry for Sen, sorry that he was poor, sorry that he was willing to steal.

"Aren't you even going to give him a scolding?" asked Wang in disgust. "Better go to his house with me and give him a good raking over the coals."

"What use, what use? Hurt a neighbor's feelings just for a duck? That would be foolish indeed."

By this time the Miser King had begun to feel an itching all over his body. The feathers had begun hurting again, and he was frightened once more. He became excited and threw himself on the floor in front of Mr. Lin.

"Hey! what's the matter, man?" cried Lin, thinking Wang was in a fit. "What's the matter? Are you ill?"

"Yes, very ill," wailed Wang. "Mr. Lin, I'm a bad man, and I may as well own it at once and be done with it. There is no use trying to dodge the truth or hide a fault. I stole your duck last night, and today I came sneaking over here and tried to put the thing off on old Sen."

"Yes, I knew it," answered Lin. "I saw you carrying the duck off under your garment. Why did you come to see me at all if you thought I did not know you were guilty?"

"Only wait, and I'll tell you everything," said Wang, bowing still lower. "After I had boiled your duck and eaten it, I went to bed. Pretty soon I felt an itching all over my body. I could not sleep and in the morning I found that I had a thick growth of duck's feathers from head to foot. The more I pulled them out, the thicker they grew in. I could hardly keep from screaming. I took to my bed, and after I had tossed about for hours a fairy came and told me that I could never get rid of my trouble unless I got you to give me a thorough scolding. Here is the money for your duck. Now for the love of mercy, scold, and do it quickly, for I can't stand the pain much longer."

Wang was groveling in the dirt at Lin's feet, but Lin answered him only with a loud laugh which finally burst into a roar. "Duck feathers! ha! ha! ha! and all over your body? Why, that's too good a story to believe! You'll be wanting to live in the water next. Ha! Ha! Ha!"

"Scold me! scold me!" begged Wang, "for the love of the gods scold me!"

But Lin only laughed the louder. "Pray let me see this wonderful growth of feathers first, and then we'll talk about the scolding."

Wang willingly opened his garment and showed the doubting Lin that he had been really speaking the truth.

"They must be warm," said Lin, laughing. "Winter is soon coming and you are not over fond of work. Won't they save you the trouble of wearing clothing?"

"But they make me itch so I can scarcely stand it! I feel like screaming out, the pain is so great," and again Wang got down and began to kowtow to the other; that is, he knelt and bumped his forehead against the ground.

"Be calm, my friend, and give me time to think of some good scold-words," said Lin at last. "I am not in the habit of using strong language, and very seldom lose my temper. Really you must give me time to think of what to say."

By this time Wang was in such pain that he lost all power over himself. He seized Mr. Lin by the legs crying out, "Scold me! scold me!"

Mr. Lin was now out of patience with his visitor. Besides Wang was holding him so tightly that it really felt as if Lin were being pinched by some gigantic crawfish. Suddenly Lin could hold his tongue no longer: "You lazy hound! you whelp! you turtle! you lazy, good-for-nothing creature! I wish you would hurry up and roll out of this!"

Now, in China, this is very strong language, and, with a cry of joy, Wang leaped from the ground, for he knew that Lin had scolded him. No sooner had the first hasty words been spoken than the feathers began falling from the lazy man's body, and, at last, the dreadful itching had entirely stopped. On the floor in front of Lin lay a great pile of feathers, and Wang freed from his trouble, pointed to them and said, "Thank you kindly, my dear friend, for the pretty names you have called me. You have saved my life, and, although I have paid for the duck, I wish to add to the bargain by making you a present of these handsome feathers. They will, in a measure, repay you for your splendid set of scold-words. I have learned my lesson well, I hope, and I shall go out from here a better man. Fairy Old Boy told me that I was lazy. You agree with the fairy. From this day, however, you shall see that I can bend my back like a good fellow. Goodbye, and, many thanks for your kindness."

So saying, with many low bows and polite words, Wang left the duck owner's house, a happier and a wiser man.

LUSAN, DAUGHTER OF HEAVEN

USAN went to bed without any supper, but her little heart was hungry for something more than food. She nestled up close beside her sleeping brothers, but even in their slumber they seemed to deny her that love which she craved. The gentle lapping of the water against the sides of the houseboat, music which had so often lulled her into dreamland, could not quiet her now. Scorned and treated badly by the entire family, her short life had been full of grief and shame.

Lusan's father was a fisherman. His life had been one long fight against poverty. He was ignorant and wicked. He had no more feeling of love for his wife and five children than for the street dogs of his native city. Over and over he had threatened to drown them one and all, and had been prevented from doing so only by fear of the new mandarin. His wife did not try to stop her husband when he sometimes beat the children until they fell half dead upon the deck. In fact, she herself was cruel to them, and often gave the last blow to Lusan, her only daughter. Not on one day in the little girl's memory had she escaped this daily whipping, not once had her parents pitied her.

On the night with which this story opens, not knowing that Lusan was listening, her father and mother were planning how to get rid of her.

"The mandarin cares only about boys," said he roughly. "A man might kill a dozen girls and he wouldn't say a word."

"Lusan's no good anyway," added the mother. "Our boat is small, and she's always in the wrong place."

"Yes, and it takes as much to feed her as if she were a boy. If you say so, I'll do it this very night."

"All right," she answered, "but you'd better wait until the moon has set."

"Very well, wife, we'll let the moon go down first, and then the girl."

No wonder Lusan's little heart beat fast with terror, for there could be no doubt as to the meaning of her parents' words.

At last when she heard them snoring and knew they were both sound asleep, she got up silently, dressed herself, and climbed the ladder leading to the deck. Only one thought was in her heart, to save herself by instant flight. There were no extra clothes, not a bite of food to take with her. Besides the rags on her back there was only one thing she could call her own, a tiny soapstone image of the goddess Guanyin, which she had found one day while walking in the sand. This was the only treasure and plaything of her childhood, and if she had not watched carefully, her mother would have taken even this away from her. Oh, how she had nursed this idol, and how closely she had listened to the stories an old priest had told about Guanyin the Goddess of Mercy, the best friend of women and children, to whom they might always pray in time of trouble.

It was very dark when Lusan raised the trapdoor leading to the outer air, and looked out into the night. The moon had just gone down, and frogs were croaking along the shore. Slowly and carefully she pushed against the door, for she was afraid that the wind coming in suddenly might awaken the sleepers or, worse still, cause her to let the trap fall with a bang. At last, however, she stood on the deck, alone and ready to go out into the big world. As she stepped to the side of the boat the black water did not make her feel afraid, and she went ashore without the slightest tremble.

Now she ran quickly along the bank, shrinking back into the shadows whenever she heard the noise of footsteps, and thus hiding from the passers-by. Only once did her heart quake, full of fear. A huge boat dog ran out at her barking furiously. The snarling beast, however, was not dangerous, and when he saw this trembling little girl of ten he sniffed in disgust at having noticed anyone so small, and returned to watch his gate.

Lusan had made no plans. She thought that if she could escape the death her parents had talked about, they would be delighted at her leaving them and would not look for her. It was not, then, her own people that she feared as she passed the rows of dark houses lining the shore. She had often heard her father tell of the dreadful deeds done in many of these houseboats. The darkest memory of her childhood was of the night when he had almost decided to sell her as a slave to the owner of a boat like these she was now passing. Her mother had suggested that they should wait until Lusan was a little older, for she would then be worth more money. So her father had not sold her. Lately, perhaps, he had tried and failed.

That was why she hated the river dwellers and was eager to get past their houses. On and on she sped as fast as her little legs could carry her. She would flee far away from the dark water, for she loved the bright sunshine and the land.

As Lusan ran past the last houseboat she breathed a sigh of relief and a minute later fell in a little heap upon the sand. Not until now had she noticed how lonely it was. Over there was the great city with its thousands of sleepers. Not one of them was her friend. She knew nothing of friendship, for she had had no playmates. Beyond lay the open fields, the sleeping villages, the unknown world. Ah, how tired she was! How far she had run! Soon, holding the precious image tightly in her little hand and whispering a childish prayer to Guanyin, she fell asleep.

When Lusan awoke, a cold chill ran through her body, for bending over her stood a strange person. Soon she saw to her wonder that it was a woman dressed in beautiful clothes like those worn by a princess. The child had never seen such perfect features or so fair a face. At first, conscious of her own filthy rags, she shrank back fearfully, wondering what would happen if this beautiful being should chance to touch her and thus soil those slender white fingers. As the child lay there trembling on the ground, she felt as if she would like to spring into the fairy creature's arms and beg for mercy. Only the fear that the lovely one would vanish kept her from so doing. Finally, unable to hold back any longer, the little girl, bending forward, stretched out her hand to the woman, saying, "Oh, you are so beautiful! Take this, for it must be you who lost it in the sand."

The princess took the soapstone figure, eyed it curiously, and then with a start of surprise said, "And do you know, my little creature, to whom you are thus giving your treasure?"

"No," answered the child simply, "but it is the only thing I have in all the world, and you are so lovely that I know it belongs to you. I found it on the river bank." Then a strange thing happened. The graceful, queenly woman bent over, and held out her arms to the ragged, dirty child. With a cry of joy the little one sprang forward; she had found the love for which she had been looking so long.

"My precious child, this little stone which you have kept so lovingly, and which without a thought of self you have given to me—do you know of whom it is the image?"

"Yes," answered Lusan, the color coming to her cheeks again as she snuggled up contentedly in her new friend's warm embrace, "it is the dear goddess Guanyin, she who makes the children happy."

"And has this gracious goddess brought sunshine into your life, my pretty one?" said the other, a slight flush covering her fair cheeks at the poor child's innocent words.

"Oh, yes indeed; if it had not been for her I should not have escaped tonight. My father would have killed me, but the good lady of heaven listened to my prayer and bade me stay awake. She told me to wait until he was sleeping, then to arise and leave the houseboat."

"And where are you going, Lusan, now that you have left your father? Are you not afraid to be alone here at night on the bank of this great river?"

"No, oh no! for the blessed mother will shield me. She has heard my prayers, and I know she will show me where to go."

The lady clasped Lusan still more tightly, and something glistened in her radiant eye. A teardrop rolled down her cheek and fell upon the child's head, but Lusan did not see it, for she had fallen fast asleep in her protector's arms.

When Lusan awoke, she was lying all alone on her bed in the houseboat, but, strange to say, she was not frightened at finding herself once more near her parents. A ray of sunlight came in, lighting up the child's face and telling her that a new day had dawned. At last she heard the sound of low voices, but she did not know who were the speakers. Then as the tones grew louder she knew that her parents were talking. Their speech, however, seemed to be less harsh than usual, as if they were near the bed of some sleeper whom they did not wish to wake.

"Why," said her father, "when I bent over to lift her from the bed, there was a strange light about her face. I touched her on the arm, and at once my hand hung limp as if it had been shot. Then I heard a voice whispering in my ears, 'What! would you lay your wicked hands on one who made the tears of Guanyin flow? Do you not know that when she cries the gods themselves are weeping?'"

"I too heard that voice," said the mother, her voice trembling; "I heard it, and it seemed as if a hundred wicked imps pricked me with spears, at every prick repeating these terrible words, 'And would you kill a daughter of the gods?'"

"It is strange," he added, "to think how we had begun to hate this child, when all the time she belonged to another world than ours. How wicked we must be since we could not see her goodness."

"Yes, and no doubt for every time we have struck her, a thousand blows will be given us by Yama, for our insults to the gods."

Lusan waited no longer, but rose to dress herself. Her heart was burning with love for everything around her. She would tell her parents that she forgave them, tell them how she loved them still in spite of all their wickedness. To her surprise the ragged clothes were nowhere to be seen. In place of them she found on one side of the bed the most beautiful garments. The softest of silks, bright with flowers—so lovely that she fancied they must have been taken from the garden of the gods—were ready to slip on her little body. As she dressed herself she saw with surprise that her fingers were shapely, that her skin was soft and smooth. Only the day before, her hands had been rough and cracked by hard work and the cold of winter. More and more amazed, she stooped to put on her shoes. Instead of the worn-out soiled shoes of yesterday, the prettiest little satin slippers were there all ready for her tiny feet.

As she dressed herself she saw with surprise that her fingers were shapely.

Finally she climbed the rude ladder, and lo, everything she touched seemed to be changed as if by magic, like her gown. The narrow rungs of the ladder had become broad steps of polished wood, and it seemed as if she was mounting the polished stairway of some fairy-built pagoda. When she reached the deck everything was changed. The ragged patchwork which had served so long as a sail had become a beautiful sheet of canvas that rolled and floated proudly in the river breeze. Below were the dirty fishing boats which Lusan was used to, but here was a stately ship, larger and fairer than any she had ever dreamed of, a ship which had sprung into being as if at the touch of her feet.

After searching several minutes for her parents she found them trembling in a corner, with a look of great fear on their faces. They were clad in rags, as usual, and in no way changed except that their savage faces seemed to have become a trifle softened. Lusan drew near the wretched group and bowed low before them.

Her mother tried to speak; her lips moved, but made no sound: she had been struck dumb with fear.

"A goddess, a goddess!" murmured the father, bending forward three times and knocking his head on the deck. As for the brothers, they hid their faces in their hands as if dazzled by a sudden burst of sunlight.

For a moment Lusan paused. Then, stretching out her hand, she touched her father on the shoulder. "Do you not know me, father? It is Lusan, your little daughter."

The man looked at her in wonder. His whole body shook, his lips trembled, his hard brutish face had on it a strange light. Suddenly he bent far over and touched his forehead to her feet. Mother and sons followed his example. Then all gazed at her as if waiting for her command.

"Speak, father," said Lusan. "Tell me that you love me, say that you will not kill your child."

"Daughter of the gods, and not of mine," he mumbled, and then paused as if afraid to continue.

"What is it, father? Have no fear."

"First, tell me that you forgive me."

The child put her left hand upon her father's forehead and held the right above the heads of the others, "As the Goddess of Mercy has given me her favor, so I in her name bestow on you the love of heaven. Live in peace, my parents. Brothers, speak no angry words. Oh, my dear ones, let joy be yours forever. When only love shall rule your lives, this ship is yours and all that is in it."

Thus did Lusan change her loved ones. The miserable family which had lived in poverty now found itself enjoying peace and happiness. At first they did not know how to live as Lusan had directed. The father sometimes lost his temper and the mother spoke spiteful words; but as they grew in wisdom and courage they soon began to see that only love must rule.

All this time the great boat was moving up and down the river. Its company of sailors obeyed Lusan's slightest wish. When their nets were cast overboard they were always drawn back full of the largest, choicest fish. These fish were sold at the city markets, and soon people began to say that Lusan was the richest person in the whole country.

One beautiful day during the Second Moon, the family had just returned from the temple. It was Guanyin's birthday, and, led by Lusan, they had gone gladly to do the goddess honor. They had just mounted to the vessel's deck when Lusan's father, who had been looking off towards the west, suddenly called the family to his side. "See!" he exclaimed. "What kind of bird is that yonder in the sky?"

As they looked, they saw that the strange object was coming nearer and nearer, and directly towards the ship. Everyone was excited except Lusan. She was calm, as if waiting for something she had long expected.

"It is a flight of doves," cried the father in astonishment, "and they seem to be drawing something through the air."

At last, as the birds flew right over the vessel, the surprised onlookers saw that floating beneath their wings was a wonderful chair, all white and gold, more dazzling even than the one they had dreamed the emperor himself sat in on the Dragon Throne. Around each snow-white neck was fastened a long streamer of pure gold, and these silken ribbons were tied to the chair in such a manner as to hold it floating wherever its light-winged coursers chose to fly.

Down, down, over the magic vessel came the empty chair, and as it descended, a shower of pure white lilies fell about the feet of Lusan, until she, the queen of all the flowers, was almost buried. The doves hovered above her head for an instant, and then gently lowered their burden until it was just in front of her.

With a farewell wave to her father and mother, Lusan stepped into the fairy car. As the birds began to rise, a voice from the clouds spoke in tones of softest music: "Thus Guanyin, Mother of Mercies, rewards Lusan, daughter of the earth. Out of the dust spring the flowers; out of the soil comes goodness. Lusan! that tear which you drew from Guanyin's eye fell upon the dry ground and softened it; it touched the hearts of those who loved you not. Daughter of earth no longer, rise into the Western Heaven, there to take your place among the fairies, there to be a star within the azure realms above."

As Lusan's doves disappeared in the distant skies, a rosy light surrounded her flying car. It seemed to those who gazed in wonder that heaven's gates were opening to receive her. At last when she was gone beyond their sight, suddenly it grew dark upon the earth, and the eyes of all that looked were wet with tears.